DEATH
OF A MINOR CHARACTER

By E. X. Ferrars

DEATH
OF A MINOR CHARACTER

E. X. FERRARS

PUBLISHED FOR THE CRIME CLUB BY
DOUBLEDAY & COMPANY, INC.
GARDEN CITY, NEW YORK
1983

All of the characters in this book
are fictitious, and any resemblance
to actual persons, living or dead,
is purely coincidental.

Library of Congress Cataloging in Publication Data

Ferrars, E. X.
Death of a minor character.

I. Title.
PR6003.R458D4 1983   823'.912
ISBN 0-385-18839-0
Library of Congress Catalog Card Number 82-23479

11.95

DEATH
OF A MINOR CHARACTER

CHAPTER 1

I was sitting at breakfast in my dressing-gown, drinking my third cup of coffee and reading the newspaper, when the telephone rang and I had an instant premonition that the call was from my ex-husband, Felix. I often have these premonitions and occasionally they actually turn out to be right. Those, naturally, are the ones that I remember. When they are wrong I simply forget them. This time, I am not sure why, I felt sure it was Felix.

Not that I ought to call him my ex-husband. Legally we were still married. Although we had been separated for over six years, we had never got around to having a divorce. I had often thought that we should do so. It would have tidied things up. But Felix had always had a profound objection to having anything to do with the law. In a quiet but dogged fashion he resisted all forms of authority. And anyway, since neither of us had yet wanted to marry again, and since we had no children and neither of us was dependent on the other, it had been the easiest thing, and certainly the cheapest, to let the matter slide.

We still saw each other occasionally, and as long as those occasions did not last for too long, giving time for the real differences between us to come to the surface, I rather enjoyed seeing him. It made a change in the pleasant but fairly monotonous existence as a physiotherapist at a private clinic in the small town of Allingford, to which I had returned after the collapse of our marriage, and I suppose, as I went to answer the telephone, I was half hoping that it was Felix who was calling.

But my premonition had been wrong. It was a woman's voice that spoke.

"Virginia? It's Audrey."

She had no need to tell me that. With her strong Australian accent, it could not have been anybody else.

She went on, "Virginia, what d'you think, I've made up my mind, I'm going home."

"Home?" I said. "To Sydney?"

"That's right."

"Well, I'm sorry," I said. "I'll miss you. But I suppose I've always known you'd go sooner or later. You're sure it's what you really want to do?"

"Yes, I'm kind of sure. Yes, I think so."

"You don't sound too certain."

"Yes, I'm certain. But the thing is, you see, I'm getting married. That's a big step to take all of a sudden."

"Is it so sudden?"

"No, not really. We've known each other for ages. But in a way that's what makes it feel so queer, I mean, changing the relationship we've both been used to for so long. I've been getting scared it may only spoil things."

"I'm sure it won't and I expect you'll be very happy."

As much as Audrey Beasley's eventual return to her home, I had known that marriage was something that was bound to happen to her sooner or later. In fact, I did not know how she had managed to put it off for so long. She had the good-natured, unself-conscious warmth that drew men after her in droves. She was very good-looking, too, in a big, blonde, blue-eyed way. But she had arrived at the age of thirty without marrying, though I knew there was a man in Australia who had been trying to persuade her to come home for a long time. And now at last, I supposed, he had succeeded. Perhaps she found the age of thirty ominous and had begun to think that she could not go on forever, playing the field. She loved her work, I knew that, but she could go on with that in Australia as well as in England and married as well as single.

She was a remarkably competent nurse. I had met her about two years ago when she had been sent to Allingford by the agency for which she worked to look after a man who had had a hip joint operated on for arthritis. Soon after she arrived I had been sent to him to give him physiotherapy and, though I was ten years older than she was and superficially we had next to nothing in common, we had quickly become friends. As she had soon returned to London and I was kept fairly busy at home, we had not really seen a great deal of one another, but she sometimes came down to spend a week-end with me and was fond of long, rambling chats on the telephone, and it was true that I should miss her.

"I'll see you before I leave, shan't I, Virginia?" she said. "Could you come to London?"

"When are you leaving?" I asked.

"On Sunday."

"*This* Sunday?"

"Yes."

It was Thursday already. She had not given me much time to arrange a trip to London.

"That's rather rushing things, isn't it?" I said.

"Well, you know how it is. I've been kind of on the edge of it for a long time, and now I feel, if I don't act fast, I may change my mind or something. But listen, are you doing anything Saturday evening?"

"Not specially."

"I'm giving a little farewell party then. Just a few friends and the other people in the house. Please come, Virginia. It's the only chance we'll have of seeing each other before I leave and you're really the person I most want to have."

"The other people in the house," I said. "Then that means Felix."

It was my doing that Audrey had gone to live in the house in Little Carbery Street where Felix had kept on the flat in which he and I had lived during our brief marriage. She had told me about a year ago that she was tired of living in lodgings and was looking for a furnished flat, and only a short time before that I had had one of my occasional meetings with Felix and he had happened to mention that the young university lecturer, Peter Summerfield, who lived in the top flat in the house, was leaving to take up a three-year research fellowship in America and wanted to let the flat furnished. So it had seemed only good-natured to put Audrey in touch with Felix and the result of it had been that she had taken the flat and had been very pleased with it.

"You don't really mind that, do you?" she said. "You always seem to get on so well when I see you together."

"That's a show we put on for other people," I said. "We've never quarrelled in public."

"I've never really understood why you separated."

"Let's say I just found it embarrassing to be married to a man with no moral sense."

"I know you've told me that before, but I still don't get it. I mean, he's kind and good-tempered and generous. I know he doesn't always stick to the exact truth when he's talking about himself, but does that really matter? So many people don't. And he's given me a fabulous wedding-present. I'll show it to you when you come. You are coming, aren't you?"

"Yes, thank you, I'll come."

"Bless you, love. Come early. Come about seven. There'll be a meal of sorts."

We rang off and I went back to my interrupted breakfast and the story that I had been reading in *The Times* about a girl who had been murdered in Soho, who was thought to be connected with drug smugglers. As the paper was *The Times* there were not many gory details, it only said that the police thought a bearded man with a limp might be able to help them in their inquiries. A bearded man with a limp, I thought, that sounded a little too good to be true. I went on to read about an attempted coup in some African country, which had naturally been followed by slaughter, torture and increased repression, and about a protest march through London of several people objecting with shouting and banners to something or other, and as the sheer mindless monotony of it all began to have an irritating effect on me, I turned my thoughts to the fact that, like Felix, I must get Audrey a present.

Something small, I thought, which would not add any weight to her baggage, since she would presumably be returning to Sydney by air, but all the same I wanted it to be something rather special, because I was fond of her and I wanted it to be something that she would treasure as a reminder of our friendship and of her stay in England. Yet it must not be too expensive, because I had recently spent more than I could really afford on a new car and my bank balance was in a far from healthy state.

Sitting there for some time, I tried hard to think of something that would meet my requirements, but my mind remained blank. I am not clever at choosing presents. I never trust myself to guess what another person will like when occasion demands that it should be something more subtle than a bottle of whisky or a book token. So, pulling at my lower lip, frowning and brooding and failing to find a solution to my problem, I finally decided to pay a visit to the Averys. Something in their shop might catch my eye. I could not go there that day as my appointment book was full, but I could go tomorrow. Getting up, I took my breakfast tray to the kitchen, washed my single plate, cup and saucer under the tap and went upstairs to get dressed.

I had known Rose and Marcus Avery for about eighteen months. From the eager attention that they had shown me when I walked into their shop one day to buy some Christmas cards, I thought that perhaps I had been one of their first customers. Only a week or two before, when I had last passed the shop, which was in St. Christopher's Lane, a narrow street, almost an alley, that led out of the market square, it had still contained nothing but peculiarly revolting-looking secondhand clothes, as it had for as long as I could remember. But suddenly all of these had vanished. The window frame had been painted and the window was clean and there was nothing in it but a small, bow-fronted chest of drawers. It had little brass handles and was beautifully inlaid and, as Rose told me when we got talking presently, was an excellent piece of Biedermeier.

But the shop was not purely an antique shop. Past the chest of drawers I had been able to see displays of modern glass, pottery, books, embroideries and jewellery that looked modern, as well as the rack of Christmas cards that had taken me inside. In fact, it was a kind of shop that has become increasingly common in recent times and is sometimes called, I am not sure why, a novelty shop. I do not know if the owners of such shops ever make a living out of them. It is unusual to see customers in them and often, after a year or so, they are suddenly replaced by practical people like electricians or greengrocers. But for a little while they must represent somebody's daydream of having, perhaps in retirement, a nice little business and selling charming, tasteful things.

Where the Averys' shop was different from a good many of these was that the things in it really were charming and tasteful, and neither of them was near retirement age. Marcus was about forty and was both bald and slightly paunchy already, yet there was something eagerly youthful about his small, protuberant brown eyes, his plump, shiny cheeks and dimpled chin. Rose looked above five years younger than he did. She was a small woman with pointed, rather puckish features, green, slightly slanting, curiously melancholy eyes under arched, inquiring eyebrows and straight brown hair, which was cut in a kind of fringe all round her head, so that it looked somewhat like a lampshade. She and I had a long talk about Christmas cards, and then I had bought a book on Chinese ceramics, which is not one of my subjects and which I had had no intention of buying when I entered the shop, but somehow Rose had made it seem a good idea to do so. And then I had found myself drinking Nescafé with her and Marcus in the room behind the shop.

Since then we had drifted into a kind of friendship. They had come to my house a few times for drinks and I had been treated to more cups of Nescafé in the back room without having had to buy anything first. But they might have just what I wanted now. A visit to the shop seemed obviously indicated and next morning, at about eleven, I set out towards it. The May morning was bright and warm and the flowering cherries along Ellsworthy Street, where I lived, a street of unpretentious little Victorian houses, had come splendidly into bloom during the last few days. The cheerfulness of it put me into the sort of expansive mood in which it is easy to spend more than one can afford, but I ignored the danger signals.

For once, when I entered the shop, I was not the only customer. A tall, elderly man was in a corner of it with his back to me, examining a set of Regency dining chairs, turning them upside down and pointing out to Rose, who was attending to him, that they suffered from woodworm. Marcus came to meet me, smiling. He was wearing a high-necked black sweater and black corduroy trousers.

"You're just in time for coffee," he said. "I was just going to put the kettle on."

The Averys were always just going to put the kettle on when I arrived. Their eagerness to chat instead of attending to the business of the shop had made me wonder sometimes if they were lonely. I knew that they had come from London, but they had never talked about what had made them settle in Allingford or about any other friends they had in the town.

"Perhaps it could wait for a little," I suggested, "because for once I might be a customer, if you can find me what I want."

As soon as I had said that a new look came into Marcus's eyes. I would not say that they hardened exactly, but the friend changed swiftly into the salesman.

"I'm sure we can do that," he said. "What is it—a present for someone?"

"Yes, just that."

I went on to tell him about Audrey, but I had hardly begun when the man who was interested in the Regency chairs turned round and exclaimed, "Mrs. Freer! I thought I knew your voice."

I recognized him then. He was the man in whose house I had first met Audrey, the man who had been operated on for his arthritic hip joint, who had been my patient for a time.

"Mr. Straker," I said. "And how are you now?"

"Well, very well," he said. "I still use a stick, but that's mostly for psychological support. It gives me confidence, but I don't really need it. And how are you?"

I assured him that I also was very well. Roland Straker was one of my patients whom I had liked very much, which was not something that happened invariably. He was the even-tempered, undemanding kind who took his pain and disability as a matter of course and did not expect me to perform miracles. He was about sixty, tall and well built, with thick grey hair and bushy dark eyebrows that almost met above his singularly calm grey eyes. He lived alone except for a small, competent manservant, who I believed had been with him for years, in a big house on the edge of the town. He was obviously rich, but he never talked about himself, so I did not know if he had been a professional man or a businessman who had been successful and able to retire in luxury, or if he had inherited his wealth.

"Do you remember Audrey Beasley?" I said. "I came in here this morning to buy her a present."

"Audrey—my dear Audrey—of course I remember her," he answered with a quick smile. "What a wonderful nurse that girl was. It made one feel well just to have her about the place. I wished I'd had a good excuse to induce her to stay on longer. And what's she doing?"

"She's going back to Australia to get married," I said.

"To whom?"

"To someone she's known a long time, that's all I know about him."

"Lucky man, whoever he is." He turned to Rose. "As you'll have gathered, Mrs. Avery, Mrs. Freer and I are old friends. She helped to get me back on to my feet after an unpleasant operation. But I mustn't keep her talking if she came in here looking for a present for that charming nurse I had. Audrey . . . Yes, indeed, Audrey. One of the things I liked about her was that she never kowtowed to the doctor as English nurses so often do. She treated him with just about the same amount of courtesy as she did my man, James. And very fine courtesy that was, too. I'll have the chairs, Mrs. Avery."

"At three hundred?" Rose said quickly.

"Yes, though I'm not sure it isn't a bit much in view of that woodworm."

"It's been treated," Rose said. "You won't have any trouble with it."

"I'll give you a cheque now. When can you deliver them?"

"Any time you like. This afternoon?"

"Excellent." Mr. Straker sat down on one of the chairs that he had just bought, brought a cheque-book and pen out of a pocket and began to make out a cheque.

As he was doing it Marcus said to me, "Just what is it you're looking for, Virginia?"

"A present for this Australian girl Mr. Straker was talking about. I haven't really any ideas about it, except that it had better be small, because I don't want it to add to her luggage, and something—well, individual, if you know what I mean, because I'd like her to feel I'd given it some thought, though as she's leaving on Sunday and I only heard about it yesterday, I haven't really had much time to do it."

"Something like a snuffbox, perhaps, or a card case. We've got a beauty of a card case in mother-of-pearl."

"What does one use card cases for nowadays? No one has calling cards any more. I see it just vanishing into a drawer."

"A snuffbox then. You can keep pills in it, or saccharine tablets if you're slimming."

"I doubt if Audrey takes any pills from one year's end to the next, and I've never seen any sign that she bothered about slimming."

"What about some jewellery then? I wonder if a piece of Jasper's work would appeal to you."

Roland Straker had signed his cheque, handed it to Rose and stood up. As he reached for his stick and started towards the door of the shop I saw that he still limped a little.

"It was nice meeting you again, Mrs. Freer," he said. "Give my best wishes to Audrey, won't you, when you see her? Good-bye, Mrs. Avery."

He went out.

As the door closed behind him I asked Marcus, "Who's Jasper?"

"A friend of ours," Marcus said. "A silversmith. He does some beautiful work. We've a few of his things here."

"Are they terribly expensive? Because that's another problem, I can't afford a great deal at the moment."

"Here they are. Come and take a look at them."

There was a table in the middle of the shop, the top of which was a glass display case. Marcus drew me towards it. It contained a certain amount of Victorian jewellery which attracted me, but the prices of which I knew would be far beyond me, and also a few pieces of rather heavy silver, a ring, a pendant, a pair of ear-rings. I would have felt self-conscious in anything so massive, but I agreed that they had a kind of beauty and certainly were not commonplace and I thought that Audrey might be able to carry them off. I remembered that she often wore chunky bracelets and brooches as big as horse brasses.

I nearly chose the pendant. It was oval, with the head of a dragonlike beast finely engraved on it. But there was something about the beast that put me off. With fire belching out of its nostrils and wild eyes, it was almost sinister.

"How much are the ear-rings?" I asked.

"Thirty pounds," Marcus answered. Then, seeing my expression, he amended it. "You can have them for twenty-five."

It was rather more than I had been thinking of spending, but the cheerful mood in which I had started out that morning had lasted and, after all, to buy something of any quality at all for less than twenty-five pounds nowadays is virtually impossible, so I said, "All right, I'll have them."

"Good," Marcus said. "I'm glad you like them. Jasper's an old friend and he finds it pretty difficult, making ends meet, doing this kind of thing. I believe he knows your husband."

I had sat down on the chair where Roland Straker had sat to write his cheque and had started to make one out myself. My hand, holding my pen, tightened on it.

"He knows Felix?"

I am never happy to hear of people who know Felix, because I can never be sure what kind of treatment they have had at his hands. They may remember him as that man of great charm who was so helpful to them in some way, or he may be the man after whose visit some small treasure of theirs, something that would easily slip into a pocket, was unaccountably missing.

"I believe so," Marcus said. "Your husband came in once when Jasper happened to be here and very nearly bought a small water-colour—nothing valuable, but a rather charming thing—of the square here on a market day, but we didn't quite manage to clinch the sale."

That did not surprise me. Felix loves to appear to be on the point of making some moderately expensive purchase, but then slips away before he has had to commit himself.

"But we talked about you," Marcus went on. "I know you're separated, but he visits you sometimes, doesn't he? And because of the connection with you we asked him into the back room for coffee, and it turned out that he and Jasper live quite near each other and sometimes use the same pub. Now let's go and have some coffee ourselves."

I had handed my cheque to Marcus. From the friendly tone in which he had spoken of Felix, I deduced that the Averys had not noticed any loss in their stock after he had gone. That was a relief. Antique shops were a happy hunting ground for him. They stimulated his tendency to shop-lifting, which was one of the things about him that I had found hardest to bear. He stole things for which he had not the slightest need and often gave them away as soon as he had acquired them. He seemed to think of it more as a kind of sport than as anything criminal and had never been able to understand why it upset me so much.

Rose, Marcus and I went into the back room and Rose plugged in the electric kettle and spooned Nescafé into three mugs. She was wearing neat, dark blue trousers, a dark blue shirt and several strings of coral beads. There was a cluttered desk in the room with an old typewriter on it, a metal filing cabinet with all its drawers partly open and papers bulging out of them in what was obviously no sort of order, an old kitchen table with several cigarette burns on it, some office stools, a stack of pictures on the floor, looking as if they were waiting to be reframed, some empty cardboard boxes and a good deal of packing paper and dust everywhere. In fact, it was as unlike the neat, attractively arranged room that faced the street as possible.

Taking his mug of coffee from Rose, Marcus perched on a stool and said, "So you know old man Straker, do you?"

His high-necked sweater helped to give him the look he had of being an oversized little boy, though his pink, rather babyish face was creased with fine wrinkles.

"He was a patient of mine for a little while," I said. "I don't know him well. He isn't a man you easily get to know well. He doesn't confide in one unnecessarily."

"Well, he's rich, we know that much about him," Marcus said. "He used to be chairman of some committee for sending aid to famine-stricken countries, and he's always giving money to charities. There are notices about it sometimes in the local paper. I don't know where it comes from. I've an idea he had a grandfather who was in cotton in Manchester or somewhere like that in the days when it still paid to be in cotton. Luckily for us, he's taken to us. He's the nearest thing we've got to a regular customer. He even gives us orders for things he wants us to find for him. He's set his heart on having a Sheraton tea-table and he keeps dropping in to ask if we've found one yet. That's what he came in for this morning and as we hadn't he bought those chairs instead. My theory is he's fallen for Rose and that's why he really comes in."

Rose's puckish face crinkled in a laugh. But even when she laughed her eyes stayed grave, almost sad. "Then he's the only rich man who ever has," she said. "But that sort of thing never happens at the right time, does it? Why didn't I meet him five years ago, before you'd started dogging my footsteps? It would be so nice not to be poor."

They often talked as if they were poor and I did not think that they could be making much of a living out of the shop, yet they gave certain signs of not being short of money. Their clothes might be casual but had a certain look of expensiveness and their car was a Rover. It seemed to me probable that they had some source of income besides the shop and perhaps were only using it as a convenient way of losing money to set off against their income tax, or were just playing at shopkeeping because they were bored by having nothing else to do. But they had never hinted at anything of the kind and though I felt some curiosity about them I had never yet shown it.

But for once I indulged it. "You've been married five years, have you?" I said.

"Just about," Rose answered.

"What did you do before you came here?"

They took longer to answer the simple question than seemed necessary.

Then Rose said, "I had a dull job as a secretary with a firm of accountants and Marcus was a schoolmaster. He taught art in an East London comprehensive, where you had to know more about defending yourself than about painting, and he was as bored with it as I was with what I was doing. So one day we got the idea that what we'd really like was to do something together and that a shop might be the answer. Marcus knew quite a lot about antiques, and we've a friend in London who's got a shop, who gave us advice, and I'd a little business experience, so we pooled our resources and borrowed some money and started up here."

"What brought you to Allingford?"

"We just happened to hear this place was for sale. Someone told us about seeing it advertised, I forget who, and we knew it was a pleasant neighbourhood and it's convenient for London, without being quite a suburb."

"And you haven't regretted it?"

"Oh no. No, it's turned out just as we hoped."

It is difficult for me now to say why I did not altogether believe Rose. At the time I was hardly aware that I did not. I only had a feeling that I had somehow embarrassed her, that she had not wanted to tell me what she had. Yet what could have been less exceptionable than what she had said about herself and Marcus? The only false note in it, and I did not think about that until later, had been that they had seen the shop premises advertised, particularly if she meant that it had been in a London paper, because the seedy sort of second-hand clothes shop that the place had been before they took it over seemed unlikely to have been advertised anywhere.

Looking back, however, I am inclined to think that perhaps the three years that I had lived with Felix had made me particularly sensitive to the sound of a lie, though his lies were usually more colourful than Rose's little story. It may have been that she looked at me a little too hard while she was talking and that Marcus began to tap the floor with his shoe with an odd nervousness. But I did not ask any more questions. I finished my coffee, put the silver ear-rings, which Marcus had packed in a pretty little box, into my handbag, and set off for an appointment that I had at the Rose and Crown.

The Rose and Crown, once an old inn and now a very sophisticated restaurant, faced on to the market square. It had a Georgian façade with much older rooms with low ceilings and heavy beams at the back. My appointment was for lunch with Tim Dancey. Tim was an orthopaedic surgeon who was a consultant at the General Hospital in Jellingham, the nearest biggish town to Allingford, but who gave a certain amount of his time to the clinic where I worked. Our first meeting, about a year ago, had been professional, but since then, by degrees, we had slipped into a way of having lunch together when he was in the town, and a week ago he had asked me to marry him.

The ridiculous thing was that I had accepted him, but as I had not heard from him on the subject during the week that had passed since then, I assumed that he had been no more serious than I had. It had happened during a party which had been given to celebrate the birth of a first child by a young doctor and his wife whom we both knew and at which the drink had flowed a good deal more freely than I was used to. So being kissed by Tim rather more warmly than usual and agreeing with him that a honeymoon in the Caribbean was just what we should both enjoy had seemed perfectly sensible, though by the next morning I had not really felt sure that any of it had happened. Tim had said nothing about it when he telephoned, suggesting lunch together, so I was assuming as I went towards the Rose and Crown that the matter could be safely forgotten.

He was not there when I went into the bar and sat down at one of the small tables in it, but he arrived only a few minutes later, ordered our usual drinks and joined me. He was about my own age, a tall man, slim and always noticeably well tailored. That at least was how I thought of him. I generally thought of how well his clothes fitted him, rather than of how well built he was. He had light brown hair with a slight wave in it, brown eyes that were humorous and oddly wise, and a narrow face, rather pale, with a strong, bony chin. I knew of two women who were in love with him and each of whom was inclined to believe that he was in love with her. Agreeing with them, of course, that he was attractive, I had always been careful so far not to join their number.

Giving me my drink, sitting down beside me, kissing me, but only on the cheek, as he usually did, he convinced me without any fuss that last week's episode was not weighing on his mind. We chatted about work, about a theatre to which he had been in London, and presently, over lunch, a little to my surprise, about Roland Straker. I knew that Tim was the surgeon who had operated on him, but I had never known that they had any other connection. But now Tim told me that Mr. Straker wanted to endow a research unit into rheumatology at the General Hospital in Jellingham and that Tim was one of the people who had been asked for advice as to how it should be set up.

"Nice to have money to throw about like that," he said. "If you had it, d'you think that's the sort of way you'd spend it?"

Tim, it had always seemed to me, had plenty of money himself, at least by my standards. He lived in a modern service flat in Jellingham, had a *pied-à-terre* in London, a Jaguar, liked to spend his holidays salmon fishing on a very expensive reach of the river Oykel, and his tailor's bills must have been exorbitant. All the same, perhaps he was not in the same class as Roland Straker.

"I don't think I've ever tried to think out what I'd do if I were rich," I answered. "My daydreams always have a basis of probability."

"I wonder what you do dream about," he said, and I found the gaze of his intelligent brown eyes fixed on my face in a way that reminded me of how he had looked at me at last week's party. It was disconcerting. I was not used to that kind of glance from him. "Not that I expect you to tell me. Our dreams, our real ones—I don't mean about having lots of money and all that sort of thing—are of course too private to talk about. All the same, I wonder."

"You wouldn't find mine very interesting," I said. "I'm not an imaginative type."

"I doubt that."

"Oh, it's true."

He shook his head. "You're just afraid of your dreams. And of any feeling that goes deep. I knew that last week when I asked you to marry me."

"But you weren't serious."

"Only because I knew you wouldn't be. I could be. Try me."

I played with my coffee spoon and wished that he would talk about something else.

After a moment he went on, "It wouldn't even work, would it, if I suggested we might be lovers? It wouldn't be in you to take the thing lightly, yet you're scared of going deep in. That man, what's his name, Felix, has a lot to answer for."

"It isn't his fault."

"There you go, defending him."

"What I mean is, it isn't his fault that I can't manage to commit myself wholly again. You're quite right, the thought of it scares me. And you're worth more, Tim, than the kind of feeling I could give you."

"Aren't you ever going to get him out of your system?"

"Most of the time I don't give him a thought."

"Only when someone else tries to get near you."

"Well, what do you suggest I should do about it? He's never tried to hold on to me, you know."

" 'If thine eye offend thee, pluck it out,' " he suggested.

"That sounds rather surgical advice," I said. "What I probably need is an analyst."

"You might be right at that." He was signalling to the waiter for the bill. "You've told me Felix is a pathological liar, a con man and a thief. He conned you into marriage in the first place, didn't he?"

"I suppose so."

"You've told me he let you think he was a civil engineer, working for a big firm of contractors, when the truth was they'd never heard of him and he was really working for a very shady firm of secondhand car dealers."

"Yes, and the irony of it was that I shouldn't have minded the shady secondhand car dealers in the least if only he'd told me about them. I didn't marry him because I thought he was a civil engineer. Poor Felix, I think he was rather shocked when he found that out. He did so want to impress me."

"Oh, you were pretty badly shocked yourself at the time, you needn't pretend you weren't. What's he doing now? Is he still with the same people?"

"No, I think he got frightened when their managing director went to gaol for fraud. So far he's always managed to steer clear of the law. After he left them he was a private detective for a while, but apparently that was too sordid, even for him, and after that he managed to get quite a good job with an estate agent. I don't know if he's with them still. He's got a way of changing his jobs suddenly and quickly."

"Then you haven't seen him for some time?"

"No, though as a matter of fact . . ."

"Yes?" he said as I hesitated.

"I think I'll probably be seeing him tomorrow evening," I said. "I'm going to a party that's being given by a friend who's leaving for Australia on Sunday, and she lives in a flat in the same house as Felix. She told me he'll be there."

"And you're looking forward to it."

"I'm not. I'd far sooner not have to see him."

"I'll believe that when you really break off with him. When you do . . ." He had paid the bill and we both stood up. "When you do, if you ever do, and if you ever get back a feeling there are some men you can trust, you might give a passing thought to me. Only that isn't going to be for a long time, is it, Virginia?"

"But of course I trust you now, Tim," I said. "Absolutely."

He gave a little shake of his head and I realized, even as I said it, that although of course I would trust him absolutely if there was any question, say, of his chopping away any part of my anatomy, I had not the same trust in what he might do to my emotions if I let him. He had been right when he said Felix had a lot to answer for. I had been so wrong about him, so hopelessly mistaken, that it had miserably lamed my trust in myself.

CHAPTER 2

Little Carbery Street, where I had lived with Felix for the three years of our marriage, was a turning out of one of the streets that lead into Theobalds Road. The few of the old houses still left there were narrow-fronted and Georgian, but most of the street now consisted of tall office buildings and blocks of flats. The developers had devastated it far more effectively than the bombs of wartime, which had begun the destruction of the two dignified terraces that had once faced each other across the narrow street. During the daytime it was full of traffic, but in the evening there was no problem about parking there. It was a few minutes after seven when I arrived after the drive from Allingford, which had taken me about an hour and a quarter, and I was able to leave my car just in front of the still impressive doorway of the old house.

The street door was never locked, so when I had rung Audrey Beasley's bell I pushed it open and walked straight up the steep, shabby staircase. On the few occasions when I had visited Felix there since our separation it had always given me a faintly queasy feeling to climb those stairs. Partly this was caused by their very individual smell, a smell of mustiness, of decay, of long-forgotten meals, of inferior plumbing. It was a smell which, during the time that I had lived there, I had sometimes thought of almost with pleasure as the smell of history. But mostly, of course, my present feeling of revulsion came from the fact that there is nothing that evokes past moods and emotions as potently as our sense of smell, and it brought back the memory of the turmoil of happiness and unhappiness that I had experienced in the house in a way that almost scared me. I hurried up the stairs and past Felix's doorway as fast as I could.

When I reached the top floor where Audrey lived her door was open and she had come out on to the landing to meet me. What always struck me about her first whenever I met her was her look of incredible healthiness. Her cheeks were pink, her skin was silken, her blue eyes sparkled, her fair hair shone. She was tall and in a shapely way fairly solid, but her movements were quiet and light. This evening she was wearing a dress of cream-coloured jersey which clung to her, making the most of her elegant muscular structure, and a heavy silver brooch which looked almost as if it had been made to match the ear-rings that I had brought her.

She put her hands on my shoulders, kissed me and said, "You know, I can't think why on God's earth I'm doing this. Ever since I made up my mind to go I've been thinking I'm mad."

"You're longing to go," I answered. "You can't wait."

"Well, perhaps that's true too," she said, "though now that I'm saying good-bye to all the friends I've made here, I can hardly bear it. But of course I'll soon be back for a visit."

I thought of all the places to which I had been when I was younger and had done a fair amount of travelling, hitch-hiking and walking and cycling, because I had never had any money to do it in any other way, places with which I had fallen so immediately and warmly in love that I had been certain that I should soon be back. Yet somehow I had kept very few of the promises that I had made to myself of returning. I thought it might be a very long time before Audrey returned from the other side of the world.

"Who else is coming this evening?" I asked. "Anyone I know besides Felix?"

She considered it. "The Farrars are coming. D'you know them?"

"No."

"I thought perhaps you might because I know they've got friends in Allingford," she said. "And there's Jasper Noble. He's a friend of the Farrars and I think he and Felix know each other. In fact, come to think of it, I met him and the Farrars through Felix."

"Jasper Noble," I said. "Is he a silversmith?"

"You do know him then?"

"No, but I think I was talking about him only yesterday with those people you mentioned in Allingford. The Averys. I expect they're the people you meant when you said the Farrars had friends there."

Her hand went to the brooch that she was wearing. "Jasper made this and gave it to me as a going-away present. Do you like it? I love it. I think he does wonderful work."

"That's very lucky," I said, "because I've brought you something of his that I got from the Averys. It'll go nicely with the brooch."

She had taken me into her bedroom to shed my coat and I brought the little box with the ear-rings in it out of my hand-bag and gave it to her. She cooed with pleasure over them, put them on and preened in front of the looking-glass.

"Isn't that just wonderful?" she exclaimed. "Jasper'll be so pleased. I hope you like him. I'm very fond of him. He's very shy, but don't be put off by that. He's really a very exciting person."

She took me into her sitting-room, where a few of her guests were already assembled.

The flat, like the one on the first floor in which I had lived with Felix, consisted of only a sitting-room, a bedroom, a bathroom and small kitchen. But being on the top floor, where no doubt the servants had once been housed before the house was divided into flats, the rooms were not nearly as high as in the one inhabited by Felix and the windows were not as tall and well proportioned. They had no attractive lit-

tle wrought-iron balconies outside them, there was no panel-
ling on the walls and the fireplaces were small and plain. But
Peter Summerfield, the university lecturer now in America,
who owned the flat and had let it to Audrey, had furnished
it pleasantly with grey wall-to-wall carpeting, comfortable
chairs, well-filled bookcases and some pleasing flower prints.

There were drinks on a trolley and a meal of cold meats,
salads, trifles and jellies set out on a table. Felix was there already, superintending the drinks for Audrey.

He smiled at me, said, "Hallo," poured out a glass of anon-
ymous-looking red wine and brought it to me.

"Nice to see you," he said.

I said that it was nice to see him. For the moment that
seemed to be all we had to say to one another.

I thought that he was looking well and in some indefinable
way more prosperous than when I had seen him last. This
could not have been because of his clothes, because the light
brown suit that he was wearing was one in which I had seen
him several times before and even his dark brown silk tie was
familiar. Certainly his suit looked recently pressed, but that
was something about which he was always particular, and he
always wore expensive shoes. Yet there was something unu-
sually self-assured, almost complacent about him, which, as I
remembered it, generally meant that his world was treating
him well.

I thought that he had put on just a little weight, but he
was as good-looking as ever. Though he and I were about the
same age he was wearing, I felt, far better than I was. There
were only a few threads of grey in his fair hair and very few
lines on his face. It was almost triangular, wide at the temples, pointed at the chin, and his vivid blue eyes had curiously
drooping eyelids, which made them look almost triangular
too. His mouth was wide and friendly. In some ways it was
the least deceptive thing about him, because he was in truth a
very friendly man. All that anyone had to do to win his

friendship was to show some signs of liking him. Unfortunately this did not lead him to be in the least discriminating in his choice of friends. The people whom he used to bring home to our flat to meet me might be anything from doctors of philosophy to pickpockets.

"Are you in London for the night?" he asked, returning to me after filling glasses for a few other people. "Or are you going home?"

"Going home," I answered.

"Must you? Tomorrow's Sunday. You won't have to work. Why not spend a night in your old home? We haven't had a real talk for a long time."

A talk was genuinely all he meant. That much was clear between us.

"Oddly enough, I never much enjoy staying here, though thank you for the invitation," I said. "What are you doing with yourself these days? Are you still with the house agents?"

"Oh no, I left them some time ago. It was a boring job really. No human interest to speak of."

"What's taken its place?"

"Quite an interesting thing, but don't let's bother about it now. Come and meet some of the other people. You don't know Bob Hazell, do you? He moved into the house only a couple of months ago. He's in the second-floor flat. A very nice chap. Come and talk to him."

He took me by the elbow and steered me towards a tall, heavily built man who was stooping courteously to talk to a very small woman of about sixty. He looked about thirty-five and had a round, ruddy face with blunt features, blue eyes, a good-humoured smile and curly fair hair.

Wondering why Felix should apparently be unwilling to tell me what his present job was and immediately fearing the worst, I took in what he was telling me, that the little woman was called Lilian Pace and lived in the ground-floor flat, and that the tall man was Bob Hazell, a detective sergeant. It amused me that Felix should have a policeman for a neighbour and claim to regard him as a nice chap, because his usual attitude to the police, as it was to anyone remotely connected with the law, was that the world would be a far more comfortable place without them.

Miss Pace had straight grey hair, cut short, grey eyes and small, firm features. She was very erect and was wearing a grey skirt, a frilly white silk blouse that looked too feminine for her, and discreet little pearl ear-rings. She had the air, I thought, of the very competent secretary of someone rather important, but when we had been talking for a few minutes she told me that she had been a welfare worker and was now retired.

Felix had introduced me to her and the sergeant as his wife, which might have been awkward, but they seemed to know what the situation was.

"You don't live in London, do you?" the sergeant said.

"No, but I used to," I answered. Felix had drifted away to provide new guests with drinks. "It's some time since I moved out, but I lived here for three years. In those days there used to be medical students in the flat I believe you've got now. Very noisy. Not the best of neighbours."

Miss Pace gave a gentle little titter. "I believe the whole tone of the house has improved in recent times. I believe my flat used to be a brothel. Felix told me about it. He told me about the dreadful people you used to meet coming in and out and how the police raided the place once, or meant to, but invaded your flat instead and how you found it quite difficult to persuade them not to take you off to gaol. Things aren't nearly so colourful nowadays."

I could see that she liked the idea that her flat had once been a brothel and it had been kindly of Felix to think up this fantasy for her. In fact her predecessor had been a mild little old man who had once worked in the British Museum and whose only vice, from our point of view, had been that he had been trying to teach himself to play the oboe.

"We're going to miss Audrey," Bob Hazell said. "There aren't many like her."

"Has anyone else taken the flat?" I asked.

"Not that I know of," he answered. "Perhaps it won't be let again. I believe it belongs to some man who's gone to America for three years and he may not want to risk letting it to someone he knows nothing about. It can be a tricky thing these days getting a tenant out of a place when you want it back, if he refuses to go. It can lead to court actions and what not. That's the advantage of letting to a foreigner who's only here for a limited time."

"You wouldn't call Audrey a foreigner, would you?" Miss Pace cried. "Oh no, I could never think of her as that! I often feel she's more one of us than we are ourselves, if you know what I mean."

"All the same, she comes from a good long way off and she was sure to go home some day," the sergeant said. "If I was this university chap I'd leave the place empty."

"Oh, look, there are those nice Farrars," Miss Pace exclaimed, "and Mr. Noble with them."

The room had been filling steadily since I arrived. A majority of the other guests were youngish women who I assumed were nurses with whom Audrey had made friends during her working life, but two men had just come in at the door, following a woman who I felt instinctively could not possibly be a nurse. She looked too fragile and somehow too abstracted, as if she were only half aware of where she was. If she was a nurse, I thought, she would be the kind who gives you the wrong drugs and always be too deep in her own thoughts to answer a bell. Yet she was a beautiful young woman. She looked about twenty-two, was very slender and moved with a drooping kind of grace. She had a pale, pointed face, faintly flushed with pink on the cheekbones, and long, pale gold hair which she wore falling loose down her back. Her eyes were hazel, big and shadowed with dark lashes and with a diffident kind of vagueness about them. She was wearing a shapeless cotton dress, mostly of dark red but boldly patterned with green flowers, no stockings and sandals. Her bare feet looked rather dirty, but the toe-nails were painted red to match the dress.

Felix gave her a glass of wine, then brought her over to me to introduce us to one another, together with one of the men who had come into the room with her. They were Karen and Edmund Farrar, Felix told me. The man walked with a slight lurch, which was caused, I realized, by the fact that he had an artificial foot. He managed it so skilfully that I might not have noticed it if the shoe on it had not been totally unwrinkled, which made it look rigid and lifeless. He was about forty, was of medium height, with wide shoulders and a careless, slouching way of holding himself. He had a thin, oddly expressionless face and sandy hair which had already grown thin above his forehead. He was wearing tight-fitting black trousers and a white sweater under a green velveteen jacket.

"I believe you know friends of ours in Allingford," he said. "The Averys. Felix told us you knew them."

"Yes, I know the Averys," I said. "Not very well though. They haven't been long in Allingford."

"Somehow I gathered you were quite close friends," he said.

I did not see why it should matter to him whether we were or not, but I said, "Is that what Felix told you?"

"Was it? I'm not sure," he answered. "I know he went into their shop one day when they'd only just settled there, and he met Jasper and they found they lived quite near each other, and that's how Karen and I got to know Felix. We live quite near here too. We're also in antiques. But you say you don't really know the Averys well?"

"No, we just meet occasionally," I said.

"That shop of theirs, of course, is a new venture for them. I helped them a bit when they were starting up. There's a lot to learn in the trade."

"I think they mentioned you to me," I said.

As if the subject bored her, his wife said suddenly, "Look—Jasper made this. Isn't it fabulous?"

She held up one of her hands. They were the long, very slender kind that are often called artistic, though the hands of a real artist are usually broad and powerful. Hers were the kind that look floppily elegant but are totally useless when it comes even to unscrewing the lid of a glass jar, let alone working on anything delicate and creative. On one finger she was wearing a silver ring which consisted of a narrow band supporting a big oval medallion decorated with the head of a fire-breathing dragon, very like the one that I had seen on the pendant in the Averys' shop. The work was certainly very fine.

"Yes, marvellous," I said.

"I simply love it." Karen Farrar had a soft, breathy voice that somehow went well with her dim, diffident glance. There was something of a child about her, I thought, a child who has unintentionally strayed into the company of adults and is trying hard to act as if she does not feel lost. "I call it Tarasque," she went on. "Tarasque was a terrible dragon that was killed by St. Martha. I don't know how she killed it. Perhaps it was just with a prayer. Saints were awfully clever at killing dragons, weren't they? A lot of them went in for it."

Edmund Farrar took hold of Karen's arm above the elbow and pinched it. He pinched it quite hard and she winced slightly, then gave him a brilliant smile, as if she wanted him to think that she had enjoyed it.

"Why d'you have to talk nonsense like that?" he asked. "I don't believe it's even a dragon. It's just a design Jasper likes. He uses it quite often." He turned to me. "If you're staying in

London, I expect we could get Jasper to show you his work-shop. You'd find it interesting."

"I'm going home this evening," I said. "Perhaps another time."

Miss Pace broke in. "Now that's something I'd love to do, Mr. Farrar. I'd love to watch Mr. Noble at work. But I know he wouldn't like that. I know what artists are like. But just to see the workshop, could we arrange that sometime, d'you think?"

Edmund Farrar appeared not to have heard the question, or else he was not sufficiently interested in the little woman to bother to answer her. He addressed me again. "I've known Marcus for years. We were at the same art school together, but of course he was always far more talented than I was. How do you think he and Rose are making out with the shop?"

"I don't know at all," I answered. "I think they're quite happy, but really I don't know them at all well."

I was puzzled by his insistence on talking about the Averys, but supposed it was simply because they were the only link between himself and me and we had to find something to talk about. When strangers meet it often helps if they can find a common acquaintance. But I was pleased that Audrey came up just then and drew me away.

"I want to show you what Felix has given me," she said. "I shan't know what to do with it, but it's so pretty."

She took me back to her bedroom, opened a drawer in the dressing-table and took out what I recognized as a Victorian scent bottle. It was a narrow cylinder of blue glass with a gold base and gold stopper. It was the kind of thing, I supposed, that a Victorian lady might have carried in her reticule. It was also the kind of thing that would have slipped very easily into one of Felix's pockets while the attendant in the shop where he had acquired it was talking to another customer.

But I might be doing Felix a wrong. Perhaps he had paid

for it. He sometimes did. In any case I would not have dreamt of suggesting to Audrey that she might be in receipt of stolen property. This was partly out of consideration for her peace of mind, but more, I think, because even after all the time that we had been separated I could not help feeling a kind of protectiveness towards Felix. I did not want other people to find him out, as I had.

Then Audrey took me aback by saying, "I wonder where he nicked it," and laughed. So she understood him better than I had supposed and appeared to be more tolerant of him than I had managed to be. Why hadn't he married someone like her? I wondered. Taking the stopper out of the little bottle, she sniffed at it, then held it out to me. "I believe you can still smell the old scent," she said. "Just a trace of it. I think it's lovely."

It seemed to me too that there was just a faint hint of a perfume, elusive as an old memory that dodges about at the edges of the mind, one moment convincingly there and the next moment lost.

She put the bottle back in the drawer.

"Now let's go and talk to Jasper," she said. "He was thrilled to see you'd bought these ear-rings. He wants to meet you."

If he did, he did not show much sign of it when Audrey introduced us. He muttered that he was glad I had liked the ear-rings, shifted about from one foot to the other and looked over my shoulder, carefully avoiding meeting my eyes. At first I thought this was because he was the kind of person who will never meet another person's eyes if he can help it, but after a minute or two of discussing the fact that we both knew the Averys, a subject by which I was pretty bored by then, I realized that his gaze was simply following Audrey about the room.

His big, dark eyes had a hungry look in them and watched her with a fearful sadness. He was about her age and not as tall as she was, with a pallid, freckled face and thick, curly brown hair, which he wore rather long, tumbled around it. He would have been good-looking if he had not looked so like some indoor plant that had hardly ever been in the sunlight. He wore jeans and a not very fresh white shirt. On one wrist he was wearing a silver bracelet.

He was gulping down the not very exciting wine that Audrey had supplied far faster than anyone else there and looked as if he would have appreciated something stronger. He ate hardly anything, however. I thought that a pity, because his hungry look, it seemed to me, might be caused at least partly by the fact that he was undernourished. He looked it. Miss Pace seemed to think so too, for she tried very hard to make him accept a plate of chicken salad. In the end, with an air of irritation, he gave in, took a plate, ate about two mouthfuls, then put it down. As he was doing it the bracelet that he was wearing slid down over his hand.

I said, "That's your work, of course. May I look at it?"

He held his wrist out to me. The bracelet was made of two narrow silver chains holding together four medallions, each with the dragon's head on it that I had seen on the pendant in the Averys' shop and on Karen Farrar's ring. They were not all identical, but seemed to be slightly different aspects of the same creature.

"How interested you are in dragons," I said. "Is there any special reason for it?"

He shrugged his shoulders. "It's just a sort of trade mark."

"I believe in the Middle Ages the dragon was a symbol of sin," I said.

"Could be. Perhaps I've a guilty conscience," he said indifferently.

"What started you on them?"

"I can't remember. I think I just liked them."

"Wasn't there one that guarded the golden apples of the Hesperides? Police work, so to speak."

For the first time he seemed to bring his attention fully on to me.

"So you don't like them," he said. He sounded quite angry. "Funny, I've never thought of them as anything special. I told you, they're just a trade mark. They're getting known. Not that that means I can make a living out of them."

"Have you some other job then?"

"I do a bit of window-cleaning when I can get it, and unemployment pay sometimes comes in useful. But dragons don't mean anything special to me." He looked more put out by the thought that they might than I should have expected. "Nothing at all."

He moved away and a moment later was standing close to Audrey, absorbed in her.

The party continued as such parties do, quite agreeably but without anything very interesting happening. I had another talk with Bob Hazell. In spite of his round, commonplace face, I had a feeling that he might be a person whom it would be worth getting to know better, but that is the worst of almost all parties: you may meet a dozen people whom you think you might like to know better, but you know quite well that the chances are that you will never see them again. When I was still young enough for it I had gone to parties with the feeling that just that evening I might be going to meet the perfect friend, or even the perfect lover, but by now I did not expect anything from them, unless perhaps it was the opportunity to talk for a little with some old friend.

But that evening the only friends I had there were Audrey and Felix, and Audrey, as a hostess always is, was too busy looking after everyone to talk to anyone in particular for more than a few minutes, and Felix, as well as helping her, seemed to be so occupied exerting his charm on as many people as possible that I did not see much of him. He had always enjoyed parties far more than I did. Even a quiet little one like this exhilarated him. This evening, thinking of the drive ahead of me, I decided to leave early, and was trying to reach Audrey to wish her happiness once more and to say good-bye when Felix took me by the arm and said, "Don't go yet. The others will be leaving soon, then you can come downstairs and have some coffee."

I did not want to stay and I did not want coffee but, apart from my refusal to live with Felix, I seldom refused to do anything else that he wanted. I suppose it was an attempt in a small way to make up to him for my ruthlessness in our relationship as a whole. So I had another talk with Lilian Pace, in which she told me all over again, having apparently forgotten that she had done so already, that she lived in what had once been a brothel, and that the place sometimes gave her a strange feeling, as if there were other people in it who wanted her to communicate with them, people whom she could help if only she could get in touch with them.

"Did you have much to do with prostitutes and pimps and so on in your welfare work?" I asked.

"Just with their children sometimes," she answered, "and only when they neglected or ill-used them. I worked mostly with children, adoption, fostering and so on. Heart-breaking work it could be, too. But I get this strange feeling in my flat —I'm sensitive, you see—I mean that there's some demand being made on me that I can't meet. I've got it at the moment, you know, even in this nice room, among these nice people. Someone here is terribly unhappy, I can feel that."

She was one of the people, I thought, who feel that a claim to that kind of power gives them a special right to attention but, after all, it was a fairly safe thing to say in any roomful of people; and just then I caught sight of Jasper Noble's face and for a moment I had an eerie feeling that she was gifted with insight beyond my own understanding. He had a face that was very expressive in its pinched, pallid way, and standing beside glowing, beautiful Audrey, it revealed a degree of bitterness which I found almost embarrassing to see, as if I had been caught listening at a keyhole to something deeply private.

Of course there was really nothing private about it. If he had minded who saw what he was feeling about her departure, he could have made some attempt to hide it, instead of making a positive parade of it. All the same, I wished that I had not seen it.

Miss Pace was the first to leave. She said she had already stayed up long past her usual bedtime, said good-bye to Audrey and left. It started a break-up of the party. Edmund Farrar limped over to me and asked me to give his regards to the Averys, then he and his wife left. Jasper Noble went with them. One or two of the young women who I had thought might be nurses stayed behind to help Audrey clear up and Felix and I went down together to his flat.

He turned on lights in the living-room and left me there while he made coffee. I sat down on the Victorian sofa which he and I had found in a street market and bought for a few pounds. It had been upholstered then in hideous imitation leather which was badly split, showing its horsehair stuffing, but we had replaced it with green damask and, though it was not really comfortable, it was an elegant thing and looked well in the high, panelled room with its tall windows and finely carved marble mantelpiece. Felix had bought new curtains since I had been here last. They were of dull, almost white velvet which just now framed oblongs of the darkness of the street outside.

Coming into the room with the coffee-tray and putting it down on a table near me, he went to the windows and drew the curtains. It made the room more intimate. But he had changed a number of things in it since I had left him and it felt far less a part of me than it had once. Or else time had done its healing work at last.

"New curtains," I remarked.

"Yes. Like them?"

"They're very handsome, but they'll show the dirt. I'm not sure they were a good choice for a neighbourhood like this."

He poured out the coffee.

"If they're too much trouble they can come down," he said. "It bores me, being practical."

"Yet you keep the place wonderfully well. Have you any help?"

"A nice coloured woman from down the street comes in once a week. She's splendid, except that she helps herself to my cigarettes."

He lit a cigarette for himself and sat down at the other end of the sofa. He was a chain-smoker. There had been a time when I tried to cure him of it but, like most of my attempts to alter him in any way, it had been a complete failure. Lung cancer, heart disease and so on were things in his view which only happened to other people. Or it might be the fact, as I had sometimes thought, that he did not care a great deal what happened to him. He had a fine capacity for enjoyment and yet seemed basically indifferent to what life might do to him.

"I know, I know," he said when he saw me looking at his cigarette. "I've got the good old death wish. Isn't it terrible to know as much about ourselves as that fellow Freud made sure we should and simply not to care?"

"So you've been reading Freud, have you?"

He grinned. "Do you really think so?"

"It would surprise me." In that pleasant room, so carefully and skilfully furnished, there was not a single bookcase and the only reading matter lying about was a few newspapers and magazines. "Tell me, how did your friend Edmund Farrar lose his foot? He's too young to have been in the war."

"It was a car accident," Felix answered. "He lost his foot and his wife was killed."

"Then Karen's his second wife?"

He nodded. "Yes, they've only been married a few months."

"Was he driving the car when his wife was killed?"

"No, as a matter of fact, Marcus Avery was driving. Rose was in the car too, but neither of them was hurt, or anyway, not seriously."

"How long ago did it happen?"

"I'm not sure. Before I got to know them. I think about a year ago."

In that case it must have happened since I had got to know the Averys, but neither of them had ever mentioned it.

"He didn't waste much time getting married again," I said.

"I suppose not. I believe they'd all gone off together to an auction in the country somewhere and Marcus drove through a red light or something. I know it was his fault and he had his licence suspended and was lucky not to get into worse trouble."

It occurred to me then that it was always Rose who drove the Rover, which was something that I had never thought about before.

"But I'll tell you something," Felix went on, then paused, and I had to say, "Yes?" before he continued. "I rather wish you didn't see so much of them."

"I don't see a great deal of them," I said, "but anyway, why?"

"They aren't your sort of people."

"I don't know what you mean."

"I'm not sure that I do myself." He gave his coffee a stir, frowning at it as if it somehow perplexed him. But there was nothing wrong with it. He always made very good coffee. "It's just a feeling I have about them. Call it a hunch. There's something the matter with them. They aren't what they seem. I suppose that doesn't make sense to you."

"Oddly enough, it does," I said. "I've had the same idea about them, though I can't explain it and I rather like them.

I like them better than that man Farrar, who in a queer way gave me the same sort of feeling of not being— Oh, I don't know what I'm trying to say, except that I wouldn't trust him very far if I could help it. But I liked your policeman. You know, it's a little amusing to find you hobnobbing with the police at your time of life. You've always been so careful to steer clear of them. How much does he know about you?"

A little stiffly he asked, "Is there so much to know? You've always exaggerated my shortcomings."

"That's a nice name for them," I said, "but perhaps I have. Or perhaps you're beginning to grow out of them, though it seems to me a little late in the day for that. Did you actually pay for that pretty little scent bottle you gave Audrey?"

"If I said I had, you wouldn't believe me, would you?"

"No, there's that." I drank some coffee. "She doesn't think you did, but it doesn't seem to worry her."

"She's a sensible girl. She and I have been great friends."

"Your silversmith friend is terribly in love with her, isn't he?"

"Oh, he's always in love with someone," Felix answered. "He was crazy about Jill Farrar, so Rose once told me."

"Jill Farrar?"

"Ted's first wife."

"Did Ted know that?"

"Yes, I think so."

"But he and Jasper seem good friends."

"Well, I'm not sure if any of it's true. In a funny way Jasper seems to depend on Ted. They're always together."

"Jasper didn't like me," I said. "I said something that upset him about those dragons of his. You know, I really don't like them. There's something queerly frightening about them. They made me feel there was something a bit frightening about him too, though perhaps he's just a harmless neurotic." I held out my cup for more coffee. "But there's another man who does like me, Felix. I was thinking perhaps I ought to tell you about him. He's asked me to marry him."

Felix put his cup down so abruptly that it slopped coffee into the saucer. He stared at me. Then he stubbed out his cigarette before it was half smoked and groped blindly for another. To my astonishment I saw that his hands, as he lit it, were shaking.

"You were thinking you ought to tell me about it!" he said. "Here we were, quietly drinking coffee together and talking about Freud and other people's love affairs, and all the time you were getting ready to spring a bomb like that on me."

"Well, what's wrong with it?" I asked.

He became immensely dignified. "Nothing is wrong with it if you really want to proceed with it. I shouldn't dream of standing in your way. Who is the man?"

"A surgeon I know."

"What's he like?"

"About my age, good-looking, intelligent, rich, successful."

"Then how can you hesitate?"

"You mean you wouldn't mind a divorce?"

"I should hate a divorce. You know how I feel about divorce. The thought of a lot of lawyers going gleefully over my private affairs seems to me utterly repulsive."

"They wouldn't be gleeful about anything like that nowadays," I said. "They'd just be bored, they get so much of it."

"But it's an invasion of one's privacy. If we could simply settle this between ourselves without bringing other people into it, as I think we should be able to do, I'd have nothing against it."

Privacy was of extreme importance to Felix. There were so many things about himself that he feared to have discovered, feared even a good deal more than was necessary, for his sins, such as they were, were only venal, nor mortal. I had often thought that a stronger character than myself might have been able to cope with them.

"Anyway, why d'you have to bother about getting married?" he went on. "You aren't likely to have children at your age and you'd lose on income tax. There's a tax on respectability, I suppose you know that. And that's not as unreasonable as it sounds, because it's really quite a luxury. But why not just live with the man? That would save both of us trouble and expense."

"You wouldn't mind that?"

"I didn't say I wouldn't mind it. I was just giving you some disinterested advice." He was drawing so hard on his cigarette that the ash at the end of it was growing rapidly and finally landed on the carpet, at which he cursed quietly, because that was the kind of thing that he hated when other people did it. "Virginia, is this serious?"

"That's the worst of it, I'm not sure," I said.

"Who is it you're not sure of, him or yourself?"

"Both of us."

"Because of course I'll do anything you honestly want if you'll tell me what it is."

He looked piteous as he said it, which was a mistake on his part, because there had been a time when I had been so moved by that kind of expression on his face that I had taught myself, though painfully, to be totally unimpressed by it.

"Well, thank you," I said. "That's very nice of you. I'll let you know how things go." I stood up. "I'd better start for home now, or I'll be very late."

He did not answer, but he stood up and opened the door for me and followed me down the stairs to my car. It was only as I unlocked it and started to get into it that he said, "Remember what I said about the Averys. They aren't your sort, I'm sure of it."

"But I don't understand why," I said.

"You've never been very good at understanding other people, have you? Just occasionally you might listen to me."

"It's odd, but I sometimes do. Good night."

"Good night." He stayed waiting on the pavement until I had reached the corner of the street and we were lost to sight of one another.

I was half-way back to Allingford before it occurred to me that Felix had not told me how he had been making his living since he had left the house agents. I had forgotten to ask him about it when he were in his flat and it was obvious that he did not want me to know any more than he could help, which probably meant that it was at least on the edge of being illegal. Some day, I was afraid, it would be over the edge and sooner or later he would be caught. That thought was still upsetting.

It was about half past one when I reached home and I went straight to bed. I did not wake up until nine o'clock next morning and then I did not get up for some time. When I did I made coffee and toast and sat over them for an hour or so, reading *The Observer*. But the morning was warm and bright and tempted me outside. I spent most of it in the garden, mowing my small patch of lawn and weeding the flower-beds. There were two fine lilacs at the bottom of the garden which had just come fully into bloom and which scented the air deliciously. Pale pink clematis rioted over my garage.

I made sandwiches presently, poured out a glass of sherry, took them out to the garden, put a chair in a sunny spot and had my lunch there. Then I slipped into a pleasant doze and, when I woke with my face tingling from the sunshine, read a thriller for a while, till it began to get cool, then went indoors, wrote some letters, warmed up some stew for my supper, watched television and went early to bed. It had been a very peaceful day, the kind of day of which I never seemed able to have enough. The weather had been right, my mood had been right, and my little garden was at its best. Later I was to look back on it with a kind of ache for its calm, wondering in a puzzled way when I thought of it why such days did not occur more often.

But it was the next day that I read the news in our local paper, *The Chronicle*, that in the morning of that peaceful Sunday that I had enjoyed so much Marcus Avery had been found by his wife beaten to death in his office and that it was certainly a case of murder.

CHAPTER 3

My first reaction was one of disbelief. I felt it must be some other Marcus Avery who had been killed, not the one I knew. But that this was absurd, because the name Marcus Avery was hardly a common one, was clear to me at the same time. The two contradictory thoughts stayed alongside one another for a moment, then the second prevailed. I put the newspaper down and went to the telephone.

But at that point I ran into a new difficulty. As I had told the Farrars at Audrey's party, I really did not know the Averys well and I suddenly felt sure that if I telephoned Rose she would only find it an intrusion. No doubt she had other friends in the neighbourhood, far closer to her than I was, who were standing by her now. Besides that, I was briefly aware of an ungenerous, self-protective desire not to become involved in someone else's tragedy. It was recognition of the existence of that desire, which I disliked in myself, that made me pick up the telephone and dial her number.

A man's voice answered. A policeman, I supposed. Yet there was something familiar in it, although I could not identify it immediately. It simply stated the Averys' number and waited for me to go on.

"May I speak to Mrs. Avery, please?" I said. "That's to say, if it's convenient."

"Who is it speaking?" the man asked.

"Virginia Freer," I said. "If she doesn't want to speak to me, please don't trouble her."

"Oh, Mrs. Freer, I'm so glad you called," the man said.

"This is Roland Straker. I read the news in this morning's paper and came straight round to see if I could help in any way, but it's a woman poor Mrs. Avery needs now. I found her all alone here until the police came back a few minutes ago. She doesn't seem to have any friends in Allingford. I ought to have thought of you, but she didn't suggest it herself. She seems quite frozen, I suppose in a deep state of shock. I'm sure she oughtn't to be alone."

He spoke hurriedly and rather incoherently, his voice full of agitated concern.

"Shall I come round then?" I asked. "I can come at once."

"I think that would be a good thing—oh, wait a moment, she's here. I think she wants to speak to you."

There was a pause, then I heard Rose's voice. "Virginia?" It sounded flat and very tired.

"Yes, Rose," I said. "I've only just read the news. If I'd known about it yesterday, of course I'd have got in touch with you sooner." I thought of the happy, peaceful day that I had spent gardening, dozing, reading, sitting in the sunshine with the fragrance of lilacs in the air while Rose had been coping with sudden death and horror. "Shall I come round now? Is there anything I can do?"

"No, don't come here," she answered in the same monotonous tone. "The place has been crawling with policemen ever since yesterday, and there've been reporters too. But I'd like to talk to you. Can I come round presently? I don't know quite when. I suppose I'll have to stay here till the police go away."

"Come any time," I said. Luckily it was a day on which I did not have to go to the clinic. "Come and stay here if you like. Bring an overnight bag with you."

"Thank you, that's very kind. I'll think about it." But something in the weary voice told me that she would not stay. "If anything happens to stop me coming, I'll telephone. I mean, suppose they find out anything . . ."

"It's all right, just come if you feel like it. I'll be in all day."

"Thank you." She rang off.

It was about twelve o'clock when the Rover drew up at my gate and Rose came to my door. She had not brought any overnight case, so it seemed she had no intention of staying the night, for which I was sorry, because I hated to think of her sleeping alone in the house where her husband had been killed. The Averys lived in a flat above the shop. I had never been invited into it, which was one of the reasons why I felt that I hardly knew them. I knew nothing at all about their intimate background, just as I knew no more about their past than the few things that they had chosen to tell me. I knew that the flat must be small, because it could not be any larger than the shop and office under it, but that was the limit of my knowledge.

Rose was wearing her dark blue shirt and trousers and her strings of coral beads, just as she had been when I had seen her on Friday, with a light anorak over them. She took this off as I shut the door behind her and dropped it on a chair in my small hall. Her face had a dry, papery look and was a dead, muddy colour. I took her into the sitting-room and asked her what she would like to drink and she asked for whisky. Her voice had the same flat tone that I had heard on the telephone.

"I don't really like whisky," she said as she sat down. "I never drink it normally. But at the moment it seems the only thing. I hope it won't quarrel with all the drugs I've been given. The doctor filled me full of sedatives last night. It didn't make any difference. I didn't sleep."

"So at least you had the doctor yesterday," I said. "I was afraid you might have been quite alone. I wish you'd thought of calling me."

"You couldn't have done anything. It was that policeman who sent for the doctor, the policeman who was in charge—I suddenly fainted after he'd been questioning me for what seemed like hours, though I don't suppose it really was. I've never done such a thing in my life before. He's an odd man—the policeman, I mean. He seemed rather bored by the whole thing."

"Who is he?" I knew several of the police in the district and wondered into whose hands she had fallen.

"I think his name's Chance. He's a superintendent."

I poured out a strong whisky for her and a weaker one for myself, gave her her drink and sat down.

"I've met him," I said. "Felix and I got quite involved with him once. He's not bad. But don't let that bored manner of his fool you. It isn't real."

She leant her head against the back of her chair, holding her glass but not tasting it.

"Isn't it extraordinary how the whole course of your life can be altered from one moment to the next?" she said, sounding still as if all life had been drained out of her. "This time yesterday I was walking home from church—I go to church, you know. Marcus would never go with me, but I go almost every Sunday. I'm not exactly religious, but I like the feeling of it. And yesterday the morning was so fine and the sunshine was so warm, I was feeling—well, more at peace with the world than I usually do. I'd had some worries on my mind when I started out, but they seemed to have been smoothed out. Perhaps that ought to have been a warning. It's dangerous to feel like that. I very seldom do, you know. I nearly always feel afraid of something. But I felt this wonderful sort of contentment as I was walking home, and I went into the shop, and then—well, there he was."

"In the shop?" I said. "In the newspaper it said he'd been found in the office."

"Yes, I was going to say in the office, but I could see him as soon as I got into the shop, because the office door was open. And so nothing will ever be the same again. Just from one moment to the next. . . ." Her voice faded. She looked at the glass in her hand as if she were surprised to find it there, then took a gulp of the whisky.

"It said in the paper that he was beaten to death," I said. "Was that right?"

"Yes, but . . ." She drank some more whisky. "It wasn't all that happened. And now I feel a lot of it was my fault, because I shouldn't have gone off as I did."

It sounded as if that was all that she wanted to say. There was something final about it. Her eyelids drooped, almost as if she was dropping off to sleep, and the glass in her hand tilted so that I thought she would spill it.

At last I said, "D'you want to tell me about it, or do you just want to be quiet? If you'd like to be alone I'll go and see about getting some lunch."

She opened her eyes. "I'll tell you the rest of it. If you don't hear it from me, you'll hear it from someone else—the police, perhaps, or Mr. Straker. He came to see me. He's been very kind—oh, you know that, don't you? He answered the telephone when you rang up. He'd no reason to come, it's just the kind of man he is. I think he's a very good man, though Marcus always said people like that are all hypocrites." She paused once more. "What was I saying?"

"You said you were going to tell me the rest of what happened."

"Oh yes. Well, you see, I left for church and as I left I heard Marcus in the office, talking to someone. I should say, shouting at someone. I didn't know who it was. I'd been upstairs in the flat and I hadn't heard anyone come in. I suppose Marcus let him in, whoever he was, and took him to the office. It must have been someone he knew, but I didn't hear him say anything, so I don't know whether or not I'd have recognized his voice. I just heard Marcus shouting. And that's why I went out quietly, because I could never bear it when Marcus lost his temper. I don't suppose you ever saw it, but he'd an awful temper. He could lose all control of himself and be horribly violent. He knocked me about once or twice when we were first married. But that frightened and upset him so much afterwards that I discovered, for his own sake as much as for my own, that the best thing to do when he began to work himself up into a rage was simply to walk out and leave him to get over it. And usually he got over it quite quickly and that's why I was only a little worried yesterday as I set off for church. I thought he'd have got over it, whatever it was about, and made peace with whoever was there with him, by the time I got home. And as I was telling you, I was feeling specially good as I walked home. I think I'd actually forgotten about the shouting. I just went in and—there he was."

"Did you realize at once he was dead?"

"Oh yes, because for one thing the office and part of the shop had been wrecked, chairs overturned, papers strewn around, our glass case smashed, and he'd a lot of blood all over him. So I realized there'd been a fight and that somehow he'd been killed in it. He wasn't tough, you know. It would have been quite easy for someone reasonably strong to knock him down. And whoever had done it may have panicked and got out before anyone came, perhaps not even sure that Marcus was dead. But then I called up the police, and they were round in a few minutes. I went upstairs to the flat as soon as they came and left things to them, and presently that man Chance came up to talk to me and he told me Marcus had been killed by a violent blow on the head and had fallen against the glass showcase and broken it and that that was why there was so much blood. We'd some old brass fire-irons for sale in the shop and it was the poker that had been used to kill Marcus, but they told me there aren't any fingerprints on it."

She drew a long breath, then managed to give me one of the small, wry smiles that never reached her eyes.

"Marcus used to laugh at me for going to church, you

know," she said. "He laughed at a lot of things. He said it was a terrible waste of time. But just see how useful it was to me yesterday. It gave me a perfect alibi. The police said he'd been dead for at least half an hour when I got in. They know I couldn't have done it."

"Anyway, you couldn't have fought him all over the place, could you?" I said. "It looks as if it must have been a man."

"I suppose so."

"What about a motive?" I asked. "Have you any ideas about that?"

She did not answer at once and when she did it was not a reply to my question.

"One very peculiar thing," she said. "They found a broken silver bracelet on the floor under Marcus's body. One of those things of Jasper's, with dragons' heads on it."

"Tarasque!" I exclaimed.

She gave me a startled look, as if she thought I had taken to swearing in a foreign language.

"I'm sorry," I said. "Tarasque was the name of a very formidable dragon killed by some saint which Karen Farrar told me about. She's got a ring with the head of a dragon on it, made by Jasper Noble, and she calls it Tarasque. I saw it on Saturday evening when I went to a party in London, given by an Australian friend of mine who's going home. The Farrars and Jasper Noble were there. The Farrars are friends of yours, aren't they?"

She nodded.

"And Jasper was wearing a bracelet made of silver links holding some medallions together," I said.

She nodded again wearily without much show of interest. "That's what this one is like and, if Jasper killed Marcus in a fight, I suppose the bracelet could have been broken while they were struggling and been left behind by Jasper because Marcus had fallen on top of it and Jasper couldn't find it in his hurry to get away."

"Had he any reason to want to kill Marcus?"

"You may think it sounds rather odd, since I know him quite well, but I don't know anything about that. There were a lot of things about Marcus that I didn't know. I suppose I chose not to know them."

She had finished her drink and silently held out her glass for another. I was a little nervous of giving it to her because I did not know how it might affect her in her present state. She sounded as if she had a great urge to talk, and yet there was something remote about her, as if it were not to me that she was talking. A disconcerting thought slipped into my mind that her whole story was one that she was trying out on me, a rehearsal of what she might have to say on some more important occasion. But I had no real reason for thinking this and I did not know what it was about her that so easily roused a feeling of distrust in me. I took the glass and refilled it.

As I gave it to her, she went on, "That policeman asked me a lot of questions about Jasper when I told him he'd certainly made the bracelet. But also he wanted to know if anything had been stolen from the shop. I think he'd like the case to have been one of straightforward robbery. So I went downstairs with him and looked everywhere, but I couldn't find anything missing. But I wasn't in a state to know what I was doing. I couldn't remember what we had and I kept thinking something had been taken and then I'd find it in its proper place, and I tried to explain this to him and he said he understood perfectly and there wasn't much point in my going on just then, but the thing would be to go over everything when I was feeling more normal. And then he began at the beginning again, asking me everything he'd asked me already, and that's when I fainted. When I came to I was upstairs and a doctor was there—I'd never seen him before, we've never needed a doctor since we came here—and he gave me some pills which he said would put me to sleep, but they didn't, they only made me feel worse. I never slept a wink all night."

"Have you gone over things again since then?" I asked.

"Yes, that's what I was doing this morning when you telephoned and Roland was helping me. That's to say, he was walking round with me and making notes of everything there for me to check against the list we had of our stock. And nothing seemed to be missing."

I noticed the change from the formal Mr. Straker of some minutes before to the use of Roland.

"So really you've no idea why it happened," I said. "Not a suspicion even."

"Oh, suspicions . . . !" She said it as if her mind were clogged with them and she despised them all. "Where do suspicions get you?"

I stood up. "You're very tired. I'll get some lunch, then you can have a rest. If you feel like it we can have lunch in the garden, or would you sooner I brought a tray in here?"

She looked at me absently. "It doesn't matter. I don't mind. In the garden—that would be nice. No, in here. Anywhere. I don't mind."

Suddenly, after the stress of telling me her story in a surprisingly coherent way, she seemed to have become distracted, or else it was the second drink beginning to affect her. I decided to put some food on a tray and bring it into the sitting-room, and then, if I could, persuade her to lie down. I went out to the kitchen, made omelettes, a salad and some coffee, put it all on a tray and returned to the sitting-room.

Rose was sitting slumped in her chair with her head drooping on her chest. Her glass was on the floor beside her. She was sound asleep.

I thought at first that I would not wake her merely to eat food that she probably did not want. But I had a feeling that if she did not eat something now she might go the rest of the day without eating anything at all, and also that if she wanted to sleep she could do it more comfortably on the sofa or on a bed upstairs. So I made a slight clatter with the tray as I put it down and, when that did not rouse her, spoke her name.

In the way that hearing one's own name spoken will penetrate even deep sleep, she woke at once. But her eyes were drowsy and she looked at me blankly, taking some time to return from whatever dreary dreamland she had been exploring and recognize where she was.

"I'm sorry, I don't think I can eat anything," she said. "You shouldn't have bothered."

"Just have a try," I said. "It'll make you feel better. Did you eat anything yesterday?"

"Yes. No. I can't remember. No, I don't think I did."

"Well, you can't go on like that indefinitely. Just try this."

She took the plate I held out to her and reluctantly began to eat. I could see that the first few mouthfuls were an effort, but the rest seemed to slip down easily enough, though she looked as if she was almost unconscious that she was eating. But she was eager for the coffee.

"You're being very kind to me, Virginia," she said. "It isn't as if we're old friends. I haven't many old friends, you know. Some people seem to keep their friends for their whole lives. I don't know how they do it. Most of the people I've known seemed to slip away when I got married. I know that was partly Marcus's fault. He never seemed to want to be intimate with anyone. But it must have been my fault too. I'm— well, I'm secretive. I don't want anyone to know too much about me. You'd understand that, I expect, if I told you—no, I don't mean that." She checked herself abruptly and a faint flush crept up her neck to her pallid face.

I said nothing and after a moment she went on, speaking hurriedly, "There's nothing special to tell. I've always been like that, even when I was a child, I don't know why, unless it was because of the way I used to steal things. I used to steal my mother's make-up when I was only about ten years old

and put it on in secret in my bedroom and have daydreams of
being a famous Hollywood star. I stole money, too, from her
handbag. And of course she knew it, but she never said anything about it. I used to have a sort of wish that she'd catch
me out and punish me, but she never did, and as I got older I
grew out of it, so I suppose her way was right. What nonsense
I'm talking! You aren't interested."

I had been very interested in what I thought she had almost told me before she deliberately stopped herself and
started to ramble about her childhood.

"Have you any other friends in Allingford?" I asked.

"No, not real friends, but it doesn't matter now, because I
shan't be staying."

"Where will you go?"

"London, I expect. You can so easily lose yourself in London. That's what I want most—just to lose myself."

"You won't always feel like that."

"I think I may. I told you, I've never made a success of
friendships. I used to think marriage would be all I'd ever
want, but then—well, I know a lot about loneliness. In a way
I don't mind it. I know it makes one selfish. You don't have
to worry about anyone but yourself. All the same, it makes
you feel sort of inadequate, I suppose. Do you mind living
alone?"

"I've never thought of it as the perfect way of living," I
said, "but it's better than living with the wrong person."

She gave me a long stare, as if she were trying to read more
into this remark than its fairly simple meaning. I wondered if
she was applying it to herself, because by now I had con-
cluded that her marriage to Marcus had been far from perfect
and that the thought of leaving him and facing life alone
might sometimes have been in her mind. Yet it struck me
suddenly with a sort of shock that what she had said about
loneliness could have a quite different meaning and might
not mean that her marriage had not been happy. People can

have loneliness forced upon them for different reasons. But what was the matter with me, I wondered, that thoughts of that kind should come into my mind? Had murder a special atmosphere about it that made everything seem suspect?

As she stood up, I said, "Don't go. It must be horrible in that flat by yourself. Why don't you stay and at least have a good rest?"

"No, I think I ought to get back," she said. "The police may want me. Anyway, I've taken up enough of your time."

And nearly told me more than she had intended. It was that second whisky. I felt that that was why she suddenly wanted to leave.

She added, "But it's helped to talk. I'm very grateful."

"If you want to come again at any time, just telephone."

"Thank you, I will."

She managed another of her sad smiles. I went out to her car with her and stood at the gate for a moment, watching as she drove away.

It was about four o'clock when the police came.

Detective Superintendent Chance was a gaunt and curiously drooping, unmuscular-looking man for a policeman, whom I remembered from an earlier meeting as looking chronically tired. As I saw him from my sitting-room window come up the path to my door, his footsteps seemed to drag. I recollected that when I met him before I had had the feeling that having to talk to me bored him deeply and that he would sooner have been doing almost anything else than spend his time questioning me. This had irritated me and at first had made me want to make him pay proper attention to me by insisting on telling him a number of odd things that I happened to know, which otherwise I might have kept to myself. Of course, this remoteness of his was only a trick. He was profoundly interested in his work, and as soon as I had recognized that, the trick ceased to work. However, I reminded myself of it now as I went to open the door to him, though that was not really necessary today, because I knew nothing about the murder of Marcus Avery, assuming that that was what he had come to see me about, which I was reluctant to tell him.

His manner was formal as he greeted me. "Good afternoon, Mrs. Freer. We've met before, if you remember."

"Of course I remember," I said. "Come in."

He stepped into the hall, followed by a pink-faced, square-shouldered young man whom he introduced as Sergeant Roberts.

"This is a sad business," Mr. Chance went on, though without much sadness in his expression. It merely gave him the look of being troubled by something that interfered with other things that he would far sooner have been thinking about. "We aren't used to this kind of thing in Allingford. I believe you know of the death of Mr. Avery, don't you?"

"Yes, I read about it in this morning's *Chronicle*," I said as I led the two men into the sitting-room.

"And you've seen Mrs. Avery since then," he said.

"Yes." The three of us sat down. "Are you having her followed?"

"There was no need for that," he said. "She told us she was coming here. We've just been having another talk with her. Poor woman, she's bearing up pretty well, considering everything. A good talk with a friend was what she needed."

"And now you want me to tell you what she told me."

He gave a worried frown. "There's no need to take that tone with me, Mrs. Freer. I'm only doing my job. If I have to pry into things you feel are confidential, it can't be helped."

"Well, I don't imagine she told me anything she hasn't told you," I said. "She told me how she heard her husband shouting at someone in his office before she went off to church, but that she didn't know who it was and she didn't interfere because when her husband lost his temper she preferred to keep out of the way."

"So far as you know, had Mr. Avery a violent temper?" he asked.

"I never saw it," I said, "but then I didn't know him very well."

"Is that so?" he said. "Somehow I had the impression you were an old friend."

I was tired of explaining that I had not known the Averys long or intimately.

"I met them for the first time about eighteen months ago," I said, "soon after they'd moved into that shop of theirs. And we didn't see each other very often."

"Yet Mrs. Avery turned to you when she needed a friend."

"I think she knows hardly anyone else in Allingford."

"She knows Mr. Straker."

"Yes, that's true."

"But you didn't know them before they came here?"

"No."

"You didn't know anything about them?"

"Not a thing."

"Well, well," he said, and it sounded as if he were casting doubt on everything I had said but was saving it up to use against me later. He brought the tips of his fingers together and gazed at me over them. They were long and bony like the rest of him. "What else did Mrs. Avery tell you?"

"That she went to church and that she came back and found her husband dead and the place wrecked—oh, and that you found a broken silver bracelet under his body when you moved it."

"I was coming to that." He put a hand into a pocket, brought out a plastic envelope and held it out to me. "Have you ever seen anything like that? Don't worry about fingerprints. It's been tested already."

I opened the envelope and took out the bracelet that it contained. It consisted of four medallions, held together by narrow chains which had been broken at one place. The face of the dragon, Tarasque, as I now thought of him, snarled up at me from the medallions.

"It looks like a bracelet I saw a man called Jasper Noble wearing on Saturday evening," I said. "It was at a party in London. He's a silversmith. It's his own work."

"You're sure it's the same bracelet?"

"Of course I'm not. He may have made them by the dozen."

"True." He took the bracelet back, returned it to the envelope and put it in his pocket. "Do you know this man Noble well?"

"I've met him just once at that party and I talked to him there for about five minutes."

"Do you know some people called Farrar?"

"I met them at the same party," I said, "and talked to them for only a little while too."

"I see." He looked as if he were dismissing it as a matter of little importance. "Has Mrs. Avery ever spoken to you about what she and her husband did before they came here?"

The question gave me an odd shock. I felt that it was the most important one he had asked me yet and that while we had been talking I had been sure that sooner or later it was bound to come.

"She told me that she used to be a secretary in an accountant's office and that her husband used to teach art in an East London comprehensive." I paused, trying to read some meaning on his singularly expressionless face. "Isn't it true, or don't you know?"

"Oh, it's true, as far as it goes," he answered ambiguously. "Did she mention how long ago this was?"

"What do you mean, how long ago?"

"Well, did she tell you when they gave it up?"

"I don't think she did, but I took for granted it was just before they came here."

"Ah."

"What do you mean—ah?"

"Nothing," he said, but that was obviously untrue. "Nothing at all. Just something to check up. You've been very helpful. I'd hoped you'd be able to tell me more about the Averys' past, but I realize you can't do that. Thank you all the same."

He stood up and the pink-faced young man who had sat there silently stood up too. Suddenly he spoke. "Isn't there some yarn that if you bathe in dragon's blood nothing can harm you? There was some fellow did it, but they got him all the same."

"Siegfried," I said. "The trouble was that while he was bathing a linden leaf blew down and stuck to him, so that little bit of him didn't get covered in blood and it was through that bit that a character called Hagen speared him."

"Bad luck for him after going to all that trouble," the sergeant said. "But accidents will happen."

"Come along," the superintendent said impatiently. "We've taken up enough of Mrs. Freer's time."

He thanked me once more for my helpfulness, which seemed to me mainly imaginary, and the two men left.

I hardly know how I got through the rest of the day. Whatever I did, I could not stop thinking about Marcus. When I went out to do a little shopping, while I was catching up on some washing, while I cooked some supper, his murder cast a shadow on my thoughts that there was no escaping. Not that I tried to escape it. Almost deliberately I immersed myself in the problem of it, trying to trace the origins of the feelings I had that things had been said to me that were far more important than I had realized at the time. Little things, hints dropped, sentences left unfinished, none of which I could remember accurately, merged on the edge of my mind and gave me the feeling that I knew far more than I did.

For really I knew nothing. Mr. Chance seemed to think that the past of the Averys was important and no doubt it was, but I knew nothing definite about it. All the same, certain suspicions had begun to haunt me and as the evening passed made me grow more and more restless, getting between me and the book I was trying to read and the television I tried to watch.

I began to feel an unusual desire to talk it all over with Felix. One of the good things about talking to him was that there was never any need to fear appearing absurd. When it came to absurdity, he was always ready to go one better than I was myself. If I rang up and told him what had happened that day, he would probably come up on the spot with a ready-made solution of the whole problem, which would have no relation to the facts but would somehow sound convincing. And a solution of some sort, even if it turned out after a little further thought to be obviously mistaken, would make me feel more inclined to go to bed presently and to sleep, blotting out, at least for a time, the nagging questions that had bothered me all day. They were still not clearly defined. I did not know what answers I wanted, because I did not know what questions to ask.

Not, that is to say, until it came to the end of the nine o'clock news. There had been the usual descriptions of large-scale murder in distant parts of the world, race riots, hijackings and strikes, but then came a small domestic item. In connection with the murder of Mr. Marcus Avery in Allingford on Sunday, we were told, a man was assisting the police with their inquiries.

I switched off the television, picked up the telephone and dialled Felix's number.

"That's funny," he said as soon as he heard my voice, "I was just going to ring you. You know about the murder, I suppose."

"Of course I do," I said. "Felix, did you watch the nine o'clock news?"

"No," he said.

"Then you don't know they've arrested someone."

"What, already?"

"Well, they said a man was assisting the police in their inquiries, but that's what it means, doesn't it?"

"Usually."

"I wondered if you knew who it was—if it was Jasper Noble, for instance."

"Wait a minute," he said. "I'm not sure we aren't talking at cross purposes. You're talking about Marcus Avery's murder, I suppose."

"Well, naturally."

"Yes, of course. Yes, I'd heard they'd arrested Jasper. But you see, while you've been busy in Allingford with your murder we've had one here of our own and it happens to have put me in a bit of a quandary."

"What do you mean, you've had a murder of your own?" I asked. "Do please be sensible, Felix. I've been feeling so awful all day."

"I'm so sorry, but so have I," he said. "And I meant just what I said. We've had a murder here and it's really much more puzzling and terrible than yours. You can't possibly compete with it."

"I'm not trying to compete with anything, but I'd like to know what you're talking about."

"Just that yesterday evening poor little Lilian Pace was found choked to death in her flat. Poor, harmless, good little Miss Pace. Can you beat that for horror?"

CHAPTER 4

Briefly I did not believe him. That was automatic. Felix had a great love of drama. However, the lies that he told in aid of it tended to be fanciful and charming, not horrific. I felt a chill run through me.

"When did it happen?" I asked.

"They think it was in the late afternoon," he answered. "Bob Hazell found her. He went down to her flat in the evening to return a book she'd lent him and she didn't answer when he rang though he was fairly sure she was in. So in case she was ill or something he went and got a key she'd left with him—she'd done that because she said she was getting absentminded and was afraid of locking herself out—and he went in and found her dead. Someone had choked her with his hands. I was out at the time and when I got back the place was seething with policemen. They let me go up to my flat, but they came and questioned me later, and luckily I'd an alibi for the whole time they were interested in. I'd been to tea with a nice old couple I know, then I looked in on the Farrars, but I think they'd been quarrelling, because they obviously didn't want me to stay, so I went to the Waggoners and had a snack and a drink and got talking to one or two people and stayed on longer than I'd meant to, so my time was completely accounted for."

It was not really like Felix to spend a Sunday afternoon having tea with an old couple, however nice they were, but it was not impossible.

"Then why are you in a quandary?" I asked.

"It'd be a bit complicated to explain on the telephone, but I'd rather like to talk to you about it. You might be able to advise me. Suppose I come down to see you tomorrow."

"I'm working tomorrow."

"All day?"

"Well, I'm free at lunch-time and in the evening."

"I'll come down then and take you out to lunch."

Being taken out to lunch by Felix usually meant that I ended up paying for the meal and, as he always liked to put on a show of making a special occasion of it until he was faced by the bill, it could come expensive. And what with my recent outlay on my new car and the ear-rings for Audrey, I was not feeling generous.

"I'll give you lunch at home," I said. "Bread and cheese probably."

"Fine. About one o'clock?"

"Yes, I can be home by then."

We said good night and rang off.

There was a play on television that night that I had intended to watch, but by the time I had finished talking to Felix I had of course missed the beginning of it, and besides I found that what he had told me about Miss Pace had made me lose any inclination to watch it. The horrible facts about it had only begun to sink in when I sat down after my talk with Felix. That harmless, good little woman, he had called her, and that was how she had struck me. Perhaps she had never been very intelligent and certainly she had never been beautiful. Men, probably, had played a very small part in her life, though who could tell what dreams she had had, what losses and disappointments she had suffered, what pains she had quietly endured under the calm surface that she had presented to others? But what seemed certain about her was that she had been a kind, hard-working woman, devoted to doing her best for others, who had earned a pleasant retirement and a peaceful death. And instead she had been paid with violence and terror.

Because of my thoughts about her, I could not settle down to doing anything, so I went to bed early. But that was a mistake. I was restless and slept badly. Then, as so often happens after a night of that kind, towards morning I fell into a deep sleep which was made almost more disturbing than wakefulness by lurid dreams, and then I overslept and when I woke had to hurry dressing and gulping down some coffee to be in time for my first appointment at the clinic.

It was with a boy who had broken a leg some time before, getting knocked off his motorcycle by a car when he was trying to creep past it on the wrong side and get away ahead of it at some traffic lights. He was lucky not to have cracked his skull, but he thought himself ill used. He was peevish and loud-mouthed and always irritated me, but on the principle that that was the kind of feeling that must never be shown to a patient, I usually managed to conceal it. But this morning I snapped at him that the accident had been his own fault and that it was time for him to do some growing up. My outburst astonished me as much as it did him and we both lapsed into antagonistic silence. I was more guarded with my next patient and got through the rest of the morning without further trouble. At a quarter to one I saw the last patient out and started for home. But at the entrance to the building I met Tim Dancey.

He was on his way to the car-park, where I could see his Jaguar. He was wearing a suit that I did not remember having seen before and looked as coolly poised as usual.

"Hallo," he said. "Nice surprise. Lunch?"

"I'd like it," I said, "but I'm afraid I've got to go home. I'm expecting a visitor."

"Dinner tonight then. I've got to spend the day here. The Rose and Crown at seven?"

"I'm sorry, Tim," I said. "I'm not sure how long my visitor's likely to stay. He may even want to stay overnight." I hesitated. "It's Felix."

He put an arm round my shoulders. "My dear, you're hopeless. But if it's only Felix, why not forget about him for the time being and at least come and have a drink with me? It won't do him any harm to be kept waiting."

"The trouble is . . ." I began, then found I did not know how to go on.

He let go of me and looked into my face. "What's wrong, Virginia?"

"Well, it's about the murders," I said. "That's why Felix wanted to come down."

"What murders?"

"You mean you haven't heard about them?"

"No. Oh, come to think of it, I saw a paragraph in *The Guardian* this morning that there'd been a murder in Allingford. But d'you mean you've got somehow involved in it?" He went on looking at me with deepening concern. "It wasn't someone you knew?"

"As a matter of fact, it was."

"Oh, Lord, I'm sorry. Someone you cared about?"

"Not really. It's just very shattering to have it happen to someone one knows at all. And another horrible thing's happened. A woman who lived in the house in Little Carbery Street where I used to live with Felix and where he still lives was murdered too on Sunday afternoon only a few hours after the murder that happened here. And Felix talked about it almost as if he'd got involved in it. He didn't exactly say so, but I think it's what he's going to say. I think it's why he wants to talk to me. So I'd better be making for home."

"Yes. Oh yes. I'm sorry I didn't understand at first." We started walking towards the car-park. "All the same, you're hopeless, you know, Virginia. He's only got to find some reason for making contact with you and you'll do anything he wants. And I suppose I'd better get that fact about you into my thick head. You and he aren't really separated, you're only semi-detached."

"It really isn't so, Tim. But this seemed important."

"Something or other will always seem important. He's very cunning. Well, see you again when these murders have been solved. I realize that until then you'll be fully occupied."

He gave a somewhat sardonic laugh and went off to his car. As I went towards my own car I found myself wishing that Felix had thought of coming down to Allingford on some other day, because I would far sooner have had lunch with Tim than with him.

I was planning to give Felix, as I had told him, bread and cheese, with perhaps a bottle of burgundy to make my entertainment of him not too niggardly, but when I reached my small house in Ellsworthy Street and unlocked the door I realized at once that, as had happened so often, he had upset my plans. For one thing, I could smell cigarette smoke as soon as I opened the door, and also something much more savoury and pleasant. I went into the kitchen and found him standing at the stove, stirring something that gave off a very appetizing aroma.

I stood still in the doorway.

"How did you get in?" I demanded.

"Look, we've been into that before," he said. "This is the easiest house to break into that I've ever come across. I've got a number of keys that will cope with most things, but I don't even have to use them to get in here. A strip of plastic does the job in a minute. Seriously, I wish you'd get your lock changed. The one you've got is just asking for trouble."

"I've nothing worth stealing," I said.

"You've a television, haven't you, and a radio and an electric sewing-machine? There's a market for all those things."

"They're all insured and I've no emotional attachment to any of them. If they get stolen I'll simply replace them."

"I think that's a very immoral attitude," he said. "You're

putting temptation in the way of some poor unstable character who's probably only taken to stealing because he had one
of those unhappy childhoods we hear about. Anyway, burglar-
ies can be very unpleasant things. All sorts of things can be
smashed for no rational reason and filth dumped on the carpet and obscenities scrawled on the walls. You wouldn't like
it if that happened, I assure you."

"And I don't really like the feeling that you can get in here
whenever you happen to feel like it, so perhaps I'll take your
advice and get a new lock. You knew I'd be coming soon.
You might have had the courtesy to wait for me."

"As a matter of fact, I arrived some time ago and I didn't
see the point of waiting outside when I could get in and start
some cooking. I didn't like the sound of your threat of bread
and cheese, so I came in and got ahead."

I came a little farther into the kitchen. "What's that you're
making?"

"It's a bit of an experiment," Felix said. "I haven't tried it
before. It's the sauce for fillet steak Rossini." He picked up a
spoon, scooped up some of the sauce and tasted it, then gave
a satisfied nod. "I think it'll be all right."

"Do you mean you bought fillet steaks in London and
brought them all the way down here to cook them for our
lunch?" I asked.

Felix loved good food and was an excellent cook, but this
thoughtfulness touched me.

"Well, not exactly," he said. "My train got me to Allingford rather early, so I went shopping on my way here, because
I've had an itch to try steak Rossini for some time and I
thought this would be a good occasion for it. I never can be
bothered to cook properly if it's just for myself. And I remembered that you get your meat from that shop round the corner
and I thought you'd probably have an account there. And
they'd some very nice fillet steak and I got all the other things
at the supermarket next to them."

"So I'm paying for the steak."

"You'll find it's worth it."

"But, Felix, I can't afford fillet steak, I can't, I really can't!" I heard my voice begin to rise almost out of control. Drawing a deep breath, I somehow lowered it. "If you'd bought the steaks in London as a nice surprise for me, I'd have forgiven your breaking in, but to put them on my account *and* break in—that's too much. I can't stand it. I won't have it. You can stop what you're doing and go."

He gave me a worried look. "Do you mean you're really hard up, Virginia? I'm sorry, that never occurred to me. After all, you've got your safe job with a nice salary and you seemed to be splashing money around, buying those ear-rings of Jasper's for Audrey."

"That's partly why I'm hard up. I bought a new car recently and I bought those ear-rings and of course some other odds and ends like some new shoes which one's always impelled to buy when spring comes round. So I can't afford fillet steaks."

"Well, of course, if you will go in for such extravagances . . ." He tasted the sauce again. "But naturally if I'd understood the situation I wouldn't have bought them. All the same, let's enjoy this. It's going to be very good."

He did not offer to reimburse me for the steaks.

He went on, "What I'd do if I were you is go into the sitting-room and get yourself a drink and I'll call out when I'm ready. We can eat in here, I take it."

"Don't you want a drink yourself?" I asked.

"No, thank you, but I know you can't last long without one, so go ahead. I shan't be long."

Felix himself was a very moderate drinker and always let me know that he thought I drank too much, indeed that I was half-way to becoming an alcoholic. I had done my best to cure him of this illusion, but without success. However, I had the drink that he suggested now and as I was finishing it

heard him call out from the kitchen that our meal was ready.
Soothed by the drink, or else mellowed by the smell of the
food that he had prepared, I kept to my original plan of pro-
ducing a bottle of wine. Of course it was not at the right tem-
perature, but it showed goodwill. I sat down at the kitchen
table and he dished up.

"And now," I said as I began on the controversial steak,
"what's this quandary you're in?"

"Let's eat first," he said, "then talk seriously. One can't
talk seriously while one's eating and what I want to discuss is
very serious. You know, ever since they found poor little
Lilian I haven't been able to think of anything else until the
last half hour, when I've been cooking. That always makes
such demands on one, it generally drives everything else out
of one's head. Now I just want to think about this steak and
whether I got it right."

"It's delicious," I said. "If I was a rich woman I'd employ
you as cook, handyman and chauffeur. It was terrible bad
luck that all I could afford was a husband. By the way, you
said you came by train. Haven't you a car these days?"

"No, it isn't worth having a car in London. For the cost of
running one, you can take taxis almost all the time, if the un-
derground and buses aren't good enough for you."

"But you could afford a car if you wanted one, couldn't
you? You've got a sort of prosperous air at the moment."

"I suppose you could say I'm not doing badly."

"What at?"

"Oh, let's not bother about that now. We'll talk about it
some other time when we haven't a lot else on our minds. Incidentally, I suppose it's all right if I stay the night. I brought
a suitcase on the off chance."

I had noticed the suitcase in the hall as soon as I came into
the house.

"I assumed you were staying," I said. "But why don't you

want to tell me about the job you've got? You dodged it the other evening when I asked you."

He gave all his attention to the steak. I thought he was not going to answer. Then, frowning, he said, "I expect you'd laugh at what I'm doing and I don't feel in a mood to be laughed at. You've an awful way of laughing at all the things I think are important, and this job happens to be extremely important to me."

"But, Felix, the last thing I'd do is laugh if it's important to you," I protested. "It seems to me I've kept telling you over the years how much I hoped you'd find some job you'd really put your heart into, instead of just drifting from one thing to another."

"All the same, you'd laugh at me for what I'm trying to do."

I looked at him suspiciously. "You aren't writing a book, or something like that, are you? An autobiography you're making up as you go along for which you've managed to get an advance out of some guileless publisher."

"There you are, you see," he said. "Sarcasm. Anyway, who's ever heard of a guileless publisher? But, my dear Virginia, unless you really change your attitude, you can't expect me to tell you anything intimate about myself."

"I'm sorry—I expect you're right," I said. "All right, we'll talk about it some other time and I promise I won't laugh."

"I don't trust you," he said. "I'd like to, but from bitter experience, I can't."

"Which I could say too. How nice that we think the same about something for once."

After that we finished our steaks and the bottle of wine while I told him what I knew of Marcus's murder, though he did not appear much interested in it.

Presently we made coffee and took it into the sitting-room. Throwing himself down full length on the sofa, he lit a cigarette while I poured out the coffee, then sat down in a chair on the other side of the empty fireplace. I waited for some time for him to begin to explain why he had wanted to see me, but he only gazed up at the ceiling until at last I said, "Well?"

"Yes, well, about that quandary I'm in," he answered. "One difficulty is I don't know quite where to begin. I feel like beginning at the end, with Bob Hazell's finding Lilian's body, but I suppose it might be better if I began at the beginning, that's to say, with the last time I saw her myself, because if I hadn't seen her on Sunday I shouldn't be involved in her murder in any way. You see, it was such a fine morning, I thought I'd go for a walk. I don't take enough exercise nowadays. I'm beginning to put on weight."

"I'd noticed that," I said.

He made an impatient gesture with his cigarette. "Look, are you going to let me tell my story straight through, or are you going to keep interrupting me, because it's hard enough without that to keep it clear in my mind."

"I'm sorry," I said. It seemed to me that I was always telling Felix I was sorry. He was very adept at putting me in the wrong. "Go on."

"Very well then. As I was saying, I went out for a walk. I didn't go anywhere in particular, I just strolled about, and came home again about half past twelve and there was Lilian just ahead of me, going in at the street door, and she said she was just home from having coffee with some friends and she got her key out of her handbag and opened the door of her flat. And then she stood still there and said, 'Oh, Felix, isn't it sad, I saw that poor young man, Mr. Noble, coming down from Audrey's flat this morning as I was setting out to see my friends, and of course she wasn't there. I saw her go off by taxi about nine o'clock this morning. And I told him so and he muttered he hadn't known that.' I think those were her exact words, or near enough. And then she went on to say something about its being so obvious how madly in love with

Audrey Jasper was and that anyone could have seen on Saturday evening how desperate he was at her leaving, and that she felt there was something really tragic about his having missed her that morning. So I asked her if she was sure it was Audrey's flat he'd been up to and that he hadn't come to see me, and she said he'd told her it was Audrey's he'd been to, and that he stared at her in a very strange way and then dashed out of the house."

"But—but—" I interrupted excitedly, unable to contain myself any longer, "if she saw him in Little Carbery Street in the middle of Sunday morning, the police have arrested the wrong man. He couldn't have been down here in Allingford, murdering Marcus."

"If only you wouldn't interrupt," Felix said.

"I'm sorry," I said yet again.

"You see, that's exactly what I was coming to," he went on. "I heard about his being arrested from the Farrars when I went to see them in the early evening on Sunday. Apparently he was with them when the police came and got him. I don't know why they picked on him, but of course I knew straight away there'd been a mistake because of what Lilian had told me about seeing him in the morning."

"One of the things they've got against him," I said, "is that a silver bracelet of his, with the dragons' heads on it, was found under Marcus's body. Did you tell the Farrars there must have been a mistake?"

"No, I told you, they seemed to have been quarrelling and obviously didn't want me to stay, so I didn't. Then later on there were various other things I wanted to think out before I spoke to anyone. I almost rang you up that evening, but the more I thought about things, the more complicated they seemed to be. So in fact I haven't told anyone till now."

"But why not tell the police?" I asked. "You said they came and talked to you after you got home. Why didn't you tell them about it then?"

"But that's exactly the quandary I'm in," he said. "Ought I to do that?"

"Of course you ought."

"I'm afraid it isn't as simple as that."

"Why not?"

He stubbed out his cigarette in a saucer that I had given him to use as an ashtray and lit another.

"There are various reasons," he said. "The main one is, why should they believe me? It isn't as if I'd seen Jasper myself. I'd only have been quoting something I claimed had been said to me by someone who was dead and who couldn't corroborate that what I was saying was true."

"All the same, why should they think you weren't telling the truth about a thing like that? And when you first heard from the Farrars that Jasper had been arrested for Marcus's murder, you didn't know Miss Pace was dead and wouldn't be able to corroborate what you said. So why didn't you go to the police straight away, or go home and tell her to do that?"

He wrinkled his forehead in exasperation. And unfortunately there had been no need for me to ask the question, for it was one of Felix's peculiarities that he never expected to be believed when he was telling the truth, just as he never expected to be doubted when he was lying. My theory about it was that in his childhood his father, who must have been a bullying, brutal sort of man whom I knew Felix had hated, had stupidly punished him for lying when he had been telling the truth, but had been easily deluded by pleasingly colourful inventions. So instead of growing normally out of the tendency to tell "pretend" stories, which all small children enjoy, Felix had come to rely on them as far more reliable defences, in time of trouble, than mere dull accuracy. Also, of course, he relied on them for impressing people, in which he succeeded only too often. He had easily succeeded with me when I first knew him.

"You see, at first I assumed Lilian would have told the

police about seeing Jasper," he said, "and that there was no need for me to get mixed up with them. And then when I knew she was dead—well, you know what the police are. They'd find out Jasper was a friend of mine and they'd think I was making up the story to get him off the hook."

"All the same, it couldn't do any harm now to tell them what Miss Pace told you," I said.

"That's what I wish I was sure of," he answered.

"What's the problem?"

He turned his head to look at me at last, instead of going on staring at the ceiling. His face was so troubled that I was startled. But I did not find out what he would have said, for just then I happened to glance at my watch. It was twenty-five minutes past two and I had an appointment at two-thirty.

"I've got to go now," I said. "We can go on with this when I get back."

"Just wait a minute—"

"No, I've really got to go. I'm going to be late anyway." I snatched up my handbag and ran out to my car.

It was almost six o'clock when I returned home. Felix was where I had left him, stretched out on the sofa, and except that the smell of cigarette smoke in the room had grown stronger and the number of stubs in the saucer on the floor beside him had increased, there was no sign that he had even moved while I had been gone. It was almost possible that he had not. He had a great talent for idleness and could sometimes spend hours at a time doing nothing, lost, I had always supposed, in absorbing daydreams.

Today, when I came in, he got quickly to his feet.

"We're going out to dinner," he said. "I know if we don't you'll start talking about that bread and cheese again."

"I don't think I could face another large meal after the lunch we had," I said.

"Nonsense. We'll go to the Rose and Crown."

I opened my handbag, took out my notecase and showed him the three pound notes that it contained.

"That, Felix, is literally all I've got till I go to the bank tomorrow," I said. "If you insist on going out, you'll have to pay."

"Of course I'll pay. Whyever should you think I wouldn't?"

"Those steaks. If you'd the money to pay for them, why didn't you?"

"It never occurred to me you'd mind having them put on your account. If you've an account at a shop, the normal thing is to use it, isn't it?"

I began to laugh. In the end it was what he usually made me do. It was one of the reasons why our marriage had lasted a whole three years and why I could still endure a certain amount of his company.

"Anyway, you seem to have got over your worries," I said.

"What worries?" he asked.

"The ones that were on your mind when I left you. Have you decided yet to do the obvious thing and go to the police and tell them what Miss Pace told you? We could go to them now on our way to the Rose and Crown."

"Tomorrow," he said. "Tomorrow perhaps. There are one or two things I'd like to think out first."

That meant, I knew, that he had no intention of going to the police at all. If I pressed it that it would only be fair to Jasper for him to do so, he was capable of insisting that, if Jasper had really been in London on Sunday morning, then someone besides Miss Pace had almost certainly seen him and would be able to give him an indestructible alibi, not like the hearsay article that was all that Felix could supply. In fact, he would probably say, and he might even be right, that Jasper himself had no doubt told the police of half a dozen people who had seen him during that morning and had been set free by now.

So I did not argue any more but said that if we were going to the Rose and Crown I would like to change and went upstairs, washed, changed out of the suit that I had been wearing all day into a fairly new dress, put on fresh make-up and went downstairs again. We got into the car and drove to the Rose and Crown, left the car in the car-park behind the old building, went into it and went to the bar.

Seated at one of the little tables in it, so deep in conversation that they did not notice Felix and me come in, were Rose Avery and Roland Straker.

They did not look as if they would want anyone to join them and as the bar was L-shaped it was easy for us to sit down where they could not see us. A waitress came to take our orders for drinks and brought us menus so that we could brood over what we wanted for dinner for as long as we liked. My problem was that I honestly did not want much to eat, but Felix, having promised so definitely to pay for the meal, wanted it to be lavish.

He was saying regretfully that it was a pity that really one could not eat steak twice in a day and that perhaps we ought to see what the sole *bonne femme* was like, when I interrupted, "Felix, you know it doesn't make sense for Jasper to have gone up to Audrey's flat when it's almost certain he'd have known how early she was leaving, so assuming that what Miss Pace told you about seeing him was true, what was he really doing up there?"

Felix laid down the menu without having made up his mind what he wanted and sipped his sherry.

"That's something I was asking myself when you left me alone this afternoon," he said, "but I think the answer's quite simple. I don't believe I mentioned it, but the Farrars have just taken the flat upstairs. They told me they'd got it fixed up by cable to America when I saw them on Sunday evening. They grabbed the place the moment they heard Audrey was leaving. They're living in a fairly squalid dump at the moment and I know they've been looking for something better ever since they got married. So I should think the probability is that Jasper went up there to do some sort of odd job for them. Audrey probably simply handed over her key to them and they gave it to Jasper and he went and did whatever they wanted. It may just have been that he carried up some heavy luggage for them. Ted manages very well with that artificial foot of his, but he might not be able to cope with bulky suitcases. He's told me he sometimes finds it troublesome in his trade when he needs to move furniture around."

"If you're right," I said, "won't they have known he was going there on Sunday and have been able to give him the alibi you're so reluctant to give him?"

"Possibly. But they may not have known he was going there in the morning, or the afternoon, or when. And it doesn't solve my problem, does it?"

"Whether you can possibly satisfy your conscience, you mean, that you needn't go to the police and tell them what you think was the motive for Miss Pace's murder—because that's what's on your mind, isn't it? But you still haven't told me what you think it was."

He gave a troubled sigh, sipped some more sherry, then gave me a long and curiously inquiring look.

"Virginia, tell me something," he said. "Would you consider coming back to me if I went and got myself psychoanalyzed?"

I smothered a gasp. There had been a time when I struggled so hard to persuade him to do just that, thinking, though not very optimistically, that it was the one hope left of saving our marriage, that it would seem inconsistent now if I failed to respond with anything but enthusiasm. Yet try as I would to think of the right answer, all I managed to say was, "You couldn't possibly afford it. It's frightfully expensive, you know."

"Don't worry about that, I could manage it," he said.

"How?"

"Well, I'm not doing so badly at the moment."

"In that mysterious job of yours. But what's made you think of it all of a sudden?"

"Oh, I've got rather interested in psychology recently."

I hesitated. "You mean you're serious about this, Felix?"

As I expected, he backed out at once. "It's just something I've been turning over in my mind. I wondered if it would help me in my work. That's why I started reading it up. I didn't want you to know I was the other evening, because I knew you'd only laugh at me. But then I began to wonder if going in for it properly would affect your attitude to me in any way, but I realize there isn't much hope of that. You've written me off as impossible. Anyway, I'm not sure I've much faith in it. But I might think about it seriously if you'd like me to."

A horrible suspicion had come into my mind that Felix had managed to set himself up as some kind of phoney psychotherapist and had been reading a few of the easier works on the subject to acquire some of the jargon. If I was right, it was no wonder that he was secretive about it. But if I tried probing into the problem of whether or not I was right, the answers I should be given would not be reliable.

I was just about to say that perhaps we might talk about it again if he went ahead with the idea and seemed to be making progress, which I thought was a safe thing to say because I was sure I should hear no more about it, when a voice spoke behind me.

"Why, Mrs. Freer, I didn't see you come in."

It was Roland Straker, benign and dignified, who had come limping up to us. He and Rose appeared to be on their way to the restaurant, which meant passing close to where Felix and I were sitting, and he had just caught sight of me. I introduced him and Felix to one another. Rose, who had met Felix, nodded to him coolly and equally coolly to me. It seemed to me she wished that I had not seen her and Roland Straker together.

He appeared to have no such feeling, however. "Perhaps you and your wife would join Mrs. Avery and me for dinner, Mr. Freer," he said. "I made Mrs. Avery come out with me because I'd a feeling that if she stayed alone in that flat she might forget it's a good thing to have a meal from time to time. She took some persuading, but I won my point in the end. I generally win my point when I make up my mind to it. And you both knew her husband, didn't you, so it won't be like inflicting strangers on her? Will you join us?"

Felix had got to his feet. I expected him to accept the invitation without hesitation, for undoubtedly it meant that Roland Straker would pay for the meal. But instead of answering at once Felix gazed past the older man with a look of astonishment on his face. I turned my head to find out what he was staring at and saw Jasper Noble wandering about among the little tables in the bar, apparently trying to make up his mind at which of them he would like to sit. He chose one in a particularly dark corner and was sitting down when Felix exclaimed, "Jasper!"

He started. Evidently he had not seen us and he did not look glad to see us now. But he came over to us, muttering a rather sullen "Hallo."

"So the police have let you go," Felix said. "The Farrars told me you'd been arrested."

Jasper gave a negligent nod. He was dressed as he had been at Audrey's party, in jeans and a soiled white shirt, though he had a black anorak over it. His curling brown hair, falling forward around his pallid, hungry face, looked as if it had not been combed for some time and I doubted if he had shaved that day. Perhaps the police had not provided facilities for it.

"That's right," he said. "They brought me down here and I've spent the day talking to a character called Chance, but they'd nothing to hold me on. Some joker had left one of my bracelets under Marcus's body, that was all, and when I showed them I'd still got my own, intact, they had to admit they'd nothing else on me. A waste of their time and mine."

He thrust out his wrist and his silver bracelet slid down from under the black sleeve of his anorak. There were the four images of Tarasque, the dragon, snarling at us.

"Anyway, you'd an alibi for Sunday morning, hadn't you?" I said. "Why didn't they let you go when you told them about it?"

"Unluckily I'd no alibi," he answered. "I stayed at home the whole of Sunday morning. As a matter of fact, I stayed in bed. Alone. And naturally that was something they couldn't check up on."

In the brief silence that followed I had an uncomfortable feeling that I had known that this was what he would say. All along I had felt some doubt of the story that Felix had told me about his meeting with Miss Pace. Yet I could see no point in his having invented it.

Rose turned to Roland Straker. "I haven't introduced Jasper Noble," she said, "an old friend of Marcus's and mine. You've seen some of his jewellery."

"Yes, indeed, and very much admired it," Roland Straker said. "Will you join us for dinner, Mr. Noble? I think Mr. and Mrs. Freer are doing so."

"Oh, if you'll forgive us," Felix said quickly, "Virginia and I have to get home. I wish we could stay, but she's expecting friends later this evening." He gripped my arm above the elbow with fingers that dug into it hard. "Come along, Virginia, or that casserole you left in the oven will be ruined."

CHAPTER 5

I had not much wanted to dine out, but now that what would undoubtedly have been an excellent free meal was inexplicably being snatched away from me, I felt deprived.

"If we're going home," I said as we emerged into the car-park, "you'll have to settle for that bread and cheese."

"We aren't going to your home, except to pick up my suit-case," Felix said. "We're going to London."

"Why?"

"It's obvious, isn't it?"

"No."

"Well, let's not talk about it till I've got it clear enough in my own mind to explain it to you. I had to think fast and I think what we're doing is for the best, but there's always a chance I've got things wrong."

"I'm sure you've got them wrong."

"No, I don't think so, but just wait and see."

We got into the car and edged our way carefully out of the car-park, which had filled up a good deal since we arrived.

I knew Felix too well to try to make him talk if he was not inclined to do so. What I had not made up my mind about as we drove home was whether or not I meant to accompany him to London. It plainly had not entered his head that I might object. I think, if he had had a car of his own, I should not have done so, but he was dependent on me, or else on trains, which were not very frequent in the evening, so that by the time we reached Ellsworthy Street I knew that I was going to agree to whatever he wanted.

I even went indoors with him when we reached the house and packed an overnight bag for myself, because I had realized that, by the time we reached London and I had dropped Felix off in Little Carbery Street, I should be too tired to drive back. Little as I liked staying in the flat, it would be better than undertaking the drive when I was exhausted. With our two cases we returned to the car, got in and started the drive to London.

It was still daylight, of course, and I could see the petals of the flowering cherries along the street, shaken by a slight breeze, drifting down like a pale shower of snowflakes. Felix sat beside me, staring before him with his unfathomable expression on his face. I always believed, when I saw it, that he was seeing himself in the role of one of the great detectives of fiction, though I had never been able to decide which one it was. Perhaps it varied according to the situation. However, challenging him about it would get me nowhere. For some time, until we had left Allingford and its suburbs behind us, we drove in silence.

At last he remarked, "You're really very good to me."

"I think so too," I said.

"How many women would have set off like this without wanting chapter and verse about it before we started?"

"Very few."

"You're quite right. And I see I owe you an explanation. I thought you might see the point yourself, but it seems you haven't."

"No, but I've learnt that it's sometimes the craziest things you do that can turn out to be the most sensible."

"This isn't crazy at all, it's just common sense. Listen." He stubbed out the cigarette he had been smoking in the car's ashtray and lit another. "Lilian Pace told me she saw Jasper coming down from Audrey's flat on Sunday morning."

"Yes."

"And Marcus was killed in Allingford on Sunday morning."

"Yes."

"Yet because of that bracelet, and possibly other reasons we don't know about, the police arrested Jasper in the early evening on Sunday, before I went to see the Farrars, which I think was around six o'clock, at which time Lilian's body hadn't been discovered. So Jasper couldn't have known she was dead and there was no reason why he shouldn't have told the police straight away about her having seen him and why they shouldn't have checked on that at once instead of arresting him."

"No."

"It's true they'd have found her dead, so she wouldn't have been able to give Jasper an alibi, but how was he to know that?"

"Perhaps he knew she was dead."

"I suppose that's possible. But even then, what would have been the point of denying, as he did to us in the Rose and Crown, that he'd been out in the morning and saying he'd spent it at home in bed? It isn't as if Lilian could have been killed in the morning and he might be suspected of it. I saw her alive after he'd left."

"Mightn't he have had some reason for not wanting it known that he'd been up to Audrey's flat in the morning?"

"Exactly! And that's why we're going to London."

"To do what?"

"Oh, Virginia, you're sometimes so damnably slow! To take a look at that flat ourselves, of course, before Jasper can get back to it, and with luck before the Farrars move in. I told you they'd taken the flat, didn't I? Well, I don't know when they're moving in, but before they do I want to see what Jasper did there. It may be something quite unimportant. Or it may be something he's told the police about and that's the real reason they've let him go, though he happens not to want us to know about it. There are all kinds of possibilities. But I want to get into that flat and take a look round before anyone else does."

"How are you going to get in? Have you got a key?"

"The funny thing is, I have, so don't be afraid I'm going to break in, though that would be quite easy. They're rickety old doors with locks that are almost as bad as yours."

"How did you get the key?"

"Peter Summerfield left one with me, just as Lilian did with Bob Hazell, in case he locked himself out."

"Well, that's good, but I still don't see what business it is of ours."

"Oh, my God . . . !" He half turned in his seat and blew cigarette smoke in my face. My attention was on the road, so I did not see his expression, but I could guess from the tone of his voice that it would be impatient, irritated, yet at the same time dismayed, as if he were afraid that what he was saying was being doubted. "Don't you understand the extraordinarily difficult position I'm in now? I know what Lilian told me, but there's no one to confirm it, and if I tell the police about it after what Jasper's told them about being at home all the morning, I may get myself involved in I don't know what. And if my idea's correct that Lilian was killed because she could give Jasper an alibi, then, like her, I could be in a certain amount of danger. And I'm no hero, you know that. So it seems to me the whole thing's most positively my business, even if it isn't yours."

"I suppose she really did tell you about seeing Jasper? It isn't something you've made up?"

He gave a slight groan at what I said and looked ahead again.

"All right, if that's how you feel, let's turn round and go back to Allingford," he said.

I did not answer, but I kept on towards London. I believe it was Dr. Johnson who said that even the worst liars tell more truth than lies, and this was probably the fact about Felix.

It was dusk by the time we reached Little Carbery Street. Street lights had been turned on, but there were no lights in any of the windows of the old, narrow-fronted house. We left the car in the street before it and went up to Felix's flat, taking our suitcases with us. I took mine into the bedroom, letting Felix see that it was he who was expected to sleep on the divan in the sitting-room. He accepted the arrangement without argument. It was the kind of minor matter about which he was always amenable. But when I returned to the sitting-room he was grinning in a slightly disturbing way.

"You know, I can only offer you bread and cheese," he said.

"It's what I was expecting," I answered.

"Or I could open a tin."

"Bread and cheese will do nicely. But do we go upstairs first, or wait till we've had it?"

"Oh, we go up now, hoping, as I said, that we're ahead of the Farrars. There wouldn't be much point in going in once they're there."

"Then let's go."

He nodded, felt in a pocket for what sounded like a gigantic bundle of keys, gave a satisfied nod as if he had found what he wanted, and led the way upstairs.

He had to try several keys before he found the right one, but then the door opened and we went in.

The sitting-room was dim and full of shadows. Felix turned on the light and closed the door behind us. Audrey had left it all very tidy, which was what I would have expected of her. The place already had the impersonal air of one that is uninhabited. Chairs were placed symmetrically on either side of the fireplace. The vacuum cleaner had certainly been over the carpet since the party on Saturday. Cushions had been plumped up. Books were in perfectly straight rows in the bookcases. And already the faint film of dust that appears in any London dwelling the moment war ceases to be waged against it had become visible on all the polished surfaces. It was like a hotel room, waiting for the next guest to move in.

Felix walked forward with an odd air of caution, as if he were expecting someone to pounce out on him from behind a door or curtain. He seemed to be looking here and there, listening and even sniffing, in case there might be some telltale odour in the flat. I sat down in one of the comfortable chairs, leant back and watched.

He looked round at me. "Aren't you going to help?"

"I don't know what we're supposed to be looking for," I said.

"Nor do I. Just anything strange, anything unexpected."

"Well, luckily the man doesn't seem to have any valuables, or if he had he locked them away before he went abroad. I can't see anything here you're likely to want to pocket."

"Much chance of that I'd have with you sitting there like a watchdog!" He grinned again. "Is that why you came so willingly when I suggested we should turn back?"

"The thought was at the back of my mind," I admitted.

"You needn't have worried. I knew there was nothing here I'd covet. Anyway, you know I never let myself be tempted in the houses of friends, unless I'm quite sure they don't appreciate the charm of something they've got." He began to open the drawers of a writing-table. "Empty."

"Naturally," I said. "You wouldn't expect Audrey to leave bundles of private correspondence behind, would you, or unpaid bills?"

"I suppose not, though it's what I might easily do myself. I wonder if it's significant that she's made such a clean sweep of everything."

"It's simply that she's a tidy, efficient person. She'd never leave any disorder behind."

"You're probably right." He moved on to a corner cupboard and opened it. There were tumblers and wineglasses on the shelves. Closing the cupboard, he strolled out to the kitchen, coming back a few minutes later and saying, "The kitchen's swept clean too. Not a crumb of anything in the refrigerator. The cooker and the kettle switched off at the main. Even the dusters washed out and hung up to dry."

While he was gone a thought had been stirring in my mind that had been troubling me at intervals ever since the visit of the police the day before.

"D'you know, there's something I've been thinking about all day," I said. "Shall I tell you about it?"

He began prodding a cushion in one of the chairs, as if he thought something of interest might be hidden behind it. "Go ahead," he said.

"It's about the Averys," I said. "How much do you really know about them?"

"No more than you do."

"Yet you warned me off them."

"That was just a hunch that they weren't your sort of person."

"Really no more than that?"

"Not a thing."

"Well, apart from the murder, which of course raises all kinds of questions of motive," I said, "I can't help feeling there's something mysterious about them. Rose told me she used to be a secretary to an accountant and that Marcus was an art teacher, and I told that to the police and they asked me if she'd mentioned how long ago that was and whether she'd told me when they gave it up. I told them I'd taken for granted that it was just before they came to Allingford and Mr. Chance said, 'Ah.'"

"Just 'Ah'?"

"That's all."

"And it worries you?"

"I thought it sounded sceptical. I thought it also sounded

as if he knew things about the Averys he could have told me if he'd wanted to, but as it happened he didn't. And there's something else."

"Yes?"

"I told you, didn't I, Rose came to see me yesterday morning? I believe she very nearly told me something important about herself, but then deliberately stopped herself. But she spoke of how few friends she had in Allingford, and how she was used to loneliness, and asked me if I minded living alone."

"And you said you loved it. Yes?"

"Well, putting two and two together, and so on, I mean her reluctance to talk about herself and Marcus, and the police seeming to know about them, is it possible that for a time after they gave up their jobs and before they came to Allingford—I don't know if you'll think this hopelessly melodramatic—Marcus was in prison?"

Felix had given up his investigation of the cushions of the chair.

"I thought you were going to say that," he said.

It was a disappointment. I realized that I had hoped that he would find my idea startlingly imaginative.

"You mean you'd thought of that yourself?" I asked.

"Not exactly, no, I can't say I had. But when you suggested it I saw at once it made sense. I shouldn't be at all surprised if you're right."

"But suppose I am, what d'you suppose he'd have been in prison for?"

Felix sat down in the chair that he had been investigating, crossed his legs and lit a cigarette. Leaning back, he blew a smoke ring or two and watched them disperse. I felt as if we had taken over Audrey's flat for our own use for the evening. At last he said, "The most probable thing for an antique dealer to get into trouble about would be receiving stolen property."

"I suppose so," I said. "I know every antique dealer is afraid that things he's bought in good faith may have been stolen."

"But it's unlikely Marcus was going on with it in Allingford if the police knew his record and were keeping an eye on him."

"No, I see that."

"But if he'd been in prison it brings a new dimension into the affair."

"How?"

"Well, who knows whom he got to know there? Who knows what he may have found out? He may have picked up information which put him in a good position to blackmail somebody who turned out to be dangerous. He may have got in with a gang who decided in the end he was more of a liability than an asset and liquidated him. In any case, it's no use trying to speculate about it, because we don't know anything about the kind of people who might have been concerned. All we know for sure is that whoever did it knew he was a friend of Jasper's and tried to frame Jasper by leaving the bracelet on the scene, then killed Lilian because she could give Jasper an alibi."

"You're sure of that? You're sure that's why she was killed?"

"Doesn't it hang together?"

"It would mean that Jasper's been intended as the real victim from the start."

"Certainly. You know, somehow I've never felt very interested in Marcus's murder. I think the police will solve that easily enough. Of course, you knew him better than I did, so it may be different for you, but it's Lilian I really care about and I'll tell you why. She's somehow such a very minor character. You know what I mean. Think of all those Westerns you've watched on television when dozens of men fall off their horses, stone dead, with bullets or Indian arrows in them, and you don't give a thought to them or their poor horses either. You only worry about what's going to happen to the hero and the bad guy and the barmaid with a heart of gold, and you wait breathlessly for the final scene when right is going to triumph. It's only in very sophisticated films that it sometimes doesn't. But actually each of those dozens of corpses that littered the prairie and whom you've forgotten all about probably had a story in him that was every bit as interesting as the characters who survive to the end. D'you see what I'm trying to say? Lilian fell off her horse so very early on and the police think it's just a commonplace crime of a burglar who was scared and killed her on the spur of the moment before making off with her few quid, and they're going to give Marcus's death twice the attention they'll give hers. But it's hers that means most to me."

"That sounds rather grand, but it only brings us back to the obvious fact that you ought to tell the police about her having seen Jasper on Sunday morning."

"I've been thinking about that and I think I probably shall as soon as I've found out a little more about it myself. If I can give them a fuller story than I can at present they'll pay more attention to it." He stood up. "I haven't looked in the bedroom or the bathroom yet. Wait a minute longer, then we'll go downstairs."

He disappeared in the direction of the bedroom.

After only a minute or two he returned, shaking his head.

"Not a thing," he said. "The whole place swept as clean as a hospital. Audrey wasn't a nurse for nothing."

"So why did Jasper come up here?"

"There's only one possible conclusion."

"That Miss Pace was right and Jasper came here too late for a last glimpse of Audrey?"

"Certainly not. No, he came to remove something."

"What?"

"My guess is, money."

I shook my head. "I don't follow you. Why should Audrey leave money behind? And even if she did, how was he to know it was here, and even if he did know, why shouldn't he have told the police about coming here to get it? No, it wasn't money."

"I think it was." Felix began to walk up and down. "And I think I can think of two possible explanations of it. One is that she left some money behind which the Farrars were to use to pay some bill of hers—electricity or the telephone or something—and they happened to mention it to Jasper. It might have been as much as fifty pounds, you know. And he came here to make off with it on the quiet, so naturally he wouldn't tell the police about it. The other possibility is a bit more complicated, but I think it's the one I prefer. I think Audrey might have left some money here just for Jasper, knowing how badly he always needed it, but also that he'd be too proud to take it as a simple present from her. So she put it down somewhere in here and, either just before she left or even from the airport, phoned him to tell him where it was and that she wanted him to have it. And I suppose she'd have told him that she'd left the key under the doormat or something like that, and then she rang off before he could protest. If he even thought of protesting."

"What an imagination you've got," I said admiringly. "I could never have thought of that."

"But it fits both their characters, doesn't it?" he said. "Audrey was generous and kind and tactful. It's just the sort of way she'd have acted. And Jasper was often desperate for money, but taking it from a woman, and above all one he'd made a great parade of being in love with, may have upset his sense of dignity. But of course he'd have taken it in the end, since there wasn't much point in his refusing it when it was there, but he wouldn't have wanted to admit it to anyone else. Remember, however, he may have told the police all about it when they arrested him, and if they could check it somehow, even though they couldn't question Lilian, it may have been one of the reasons why they released him. Meantime, talking of love . . ."

"That's not on the agenda," I said.

"I wasn't going to say what you think I was," Felix answered stiffly. "I was simply going to ask you, do you think there's anything between Rose and that man Straker? Because, if there was, it might give either or both of them a reason for wanting to get rid of Marcus."

I had no answer ready for this and I should probably have said something non-committal, indicating that I had no opinion on the subject, if at that moment there had not been a knock on the door.

It was quite a gentle knock, but it made both of us start guiltily. Felix was the nearer to the door, so he went to open it. Bob Hazell stood there. He gave us a startled stare.

"Oh, it's you," he said. "I thought it might be the Farrars, but I thought I'd better come up to make sure. How did you get in?"

There was an expression of embarrassment at having caught us there, rather than of suspicion, on his face, yet I noticed that he gave a rapid look round the room before his gaze returned to Felix.

"I've had a key to the place for years," Felix said. "Summerfield gave it to me in case anything went wrong, like fire or burst pipes, when he was away. He was always going away, lecturing or going to congresses and so on. I suppose you could hear in that flat of yours that there was someone in here."

"Yes, I came in a few minutes ago and heard footsteps overhead," Bob Hazell answered. "Audrey told me the Farrars would be moving in, but I wasn't expecting them yet. What brought you up here?"

The question was very casually put, but his shrewd blue eyes were attentive.

I did not dream of trying to answer. I left it to Felix to think of something appropriate. It did not take him long.

"The fact is, a rather odd thing happened as Virginia and I got here," he said. "We were just getting out of the car—her car—you probably saw it parked outside. I was down visiting her in Allingford today and she very kindly offered to drive me home. Well, as I said, we were just getting out of the car when the street door opened and a very small old man came out. I'd say he was about eighty and he had a very severe curvature of the spine, almost a hump, and a rather big head with a surprising amount of grey hair for his age, and eyebrows—really remarkable eyebrows—and he was dressed in a very dirty old raincoat. I thought he might somehow be connected with Lilian Pace, an older brother, for instance, though he looked rather disreputable for that. And I thought for a moment he was going to speak to us, but then suddenly he turned away and scuttled off, and I didn't think much more about him till we got inside and went into my flat, when Virginia said he looked as if he were up to no good and perhaps we ought to make sure he hadn't broken into Lilian's flat, or Audrey's. So that's what we were doing. We went down to Lilian's flat first and found her door locked, and then we came up here and found the door locked too, but it just happened I'd that key of Summerfield's, so we came in to make sure everything was all right. And it is, so far as we could see."

Bob Hazell came forward into the room but left the door open behind him.

"This old man," he said, "did you happen to notice the colour of his eyes?"

Felix had the sense to say that he had not.

"Or if the bottoms of his trousers were frayed?"

"I rather think they were," Felix answered, "though I couldn't swear to it. Why?"

"Just that I've a feeling I've heard of him before. He's got a way of cropping up."

Felix looked extremely surprised, as well he might, but I thought myself that there was irony in Bob Hazell's innocent-sounding voice, and that he had not believed a word of Felix's explanation of our presence.

But if he did not, he did not pursue the matter, though he gave me a long and disconcerting look, as if he thought that he might persuade me to tell him more of the truth than Felix. Then he began to stroll round the flat himself, looking casually into the drawers of the writing-table and opening the corner cupboard, just as Felix had done, and going out to the kitchen, the bedroom and the bathroom. It was in no sense a thorough search, but only a check-up that nothing was noticeably out of order. At the same time, I presumed, he was considering what real reason Felix and I might have for being there.

Returning to the sitting-room, he said, "What about coming down to my place for a drink?"

I was feeling distinctly hungry by then and would have preferred returning to Felix's flat for the promised bread and cheese to having a drink on a very empty stomach, but Felix's relationship to Bob Hazell might possibly be important to him, so I left it to him to answer. He said enthusiastically that we should both love that and, after the sergeant had seen us out on to the landing and made sure that the door of the flat was properly closed behind us, we followed him down to his flat on the floor below.

It was the same plan as Felix's and Peter Summerfield's flats, with ceilings almost as high as Felix's and also with tall windows, though these were without the small wrought-iron balconies outside that gave elegance to Felix's. The sitting-room into which Bob Hazell took us was the room of a man who lived alone and paid very little attention to his surroundings, beyond seeing that they were kept reasonably clean. The

panelled walls were painted a drab green, long ago reduced to
dinginess by time and the London air. There was a three-
piece suite covered in brown imitation leather, with worn velvet cushions. The carpet, the most colourful thing in the
room, had a hectic pattern of reds and greens and mustard
yellow. The pictures were all prints of glittering seas and
stately sailing vessels. They suggested that Bob Hazell, while
he struggled with the squalor of crime in the London streets,
had his dreams filled with visions of sparkling blue water and
wide horizons.

The surprising thing in the room was that one wall was entirely covered with books. I had not thought of Bob as someone who was likely to be much of a reader, but rough bookcases that I thought he had probably made himself had been
built up against the wall from floor to ceiling and were entirely filled with what looked like very solid reading matter.
Here and there I saw a few paperbacks, but mostly the books
had the look of having been collected from good secondhand
bookshops. As Bob went to a sideboard on which there was a
tray of drinks and glasses, I went closer to the bookcase to see
what his interests were.

I found travel, some of it weighty stuff, such as *The Voy-
age of the Beagle* and *Arabia Deserta*, and history, economics,
jurisprudence and criminal investigation. There was almost
no fiction, no poetry and nothing that related to music or
painting. With an eye on the startling carpet in the otherwise
drab room, I thought that the sergeant's aesthetic tastes
might be deficient, but that nevertheless the bookcase was
that of a highly intelligent man.

One thing that intrigued me about it was the number of
books on psychology, from psycho-analysis to Gestalt. The
names of all but the most famous authors meant nothing to
me, since I had never got much beyond *The Psychopathology
of Everyday Life*, on the one hand, and *The Mentality of
Apes* on the other. But there was a whole shelf given over to

them and I hoped that Felix realized what kind of man he was dealing with and would not tempt Providence by giving him any more unlikely accounts of our activities.

Unfortunately he immediately did so as Bob handed him a glass of sherry, by saying, "That old man we saw downstairs, Bob—you think perhaps he's someone you know?"

Felix and I had both asked for sherry, but that had been a mistake, because Bob's taste in it was for the very sweet and sickly.

"Sounds to me like a reliable old grass of mine," he said. "He probably came to see me."

"A grass—someone who brings you information on the quiet?" Felix said.

"That's right. We all have our informants and he's about my best. Remarkable, the tips he brings me. Pity I missed him, but he'll be back again sometime if it's something important."

"That's very interesting." Felix wore a slightly bewildered air, which was only to be expected, since he must have found it strange to have one of his fictional characters taking on flesh and blood. My own belief was that he was not really doing so and that Bob was only teasing Felix. But at the same time I did not put it past Felix to have recognized this and to be playing up to Bob. The two of them were fairly well acquainted and might have their own ways of entertaining one another.

"Is it true," Felix went on, "that most important arrests are made on information received?"

"Pretty often, anyway," Bob answered.

He added something about wanting to switch his oven on to warm up his supper and went out to the kitchen, leaving us alone in the sitting-room.

I was still standing by the bookcase.

"Have you studied this?" I asked.

"Yes, Bob's a very serious chap," Felix said. "Very well informed. But not ambitious, or with his brain he'd be something more than a sergeant by now. It's the human side of police work that interests him, so he's told me, hence all those books on psychology."

"Oh, you've noticed those."

"Yes, as a matter of fact, he's been lending them to me. I told you I'd been reading it up a certain amount lately, didn't I? Well, it was Bob who got me interested in it. I'm afraid I find it pretty heavy going and yet it's got an odd sort of fascination. Once I start, I find it hard to stop. It's given me some very interesting ideas about myself and about you too. I think I understand much better than I did why you stick to me."

"But I don't," I said. "It's you who stick to me. I can't get rid of you."

"Face it, it's mutual." He had come to my side and now put an arm round me. Drawing me close, he sang softly into my ear, to a tune I vaguely remembered as having something to do with honeysuckle and a bee, "You are my super superego, I am your id." Releasing me, he started to laugh. "There—don't you agree?"

I laughed too. "I think your Bob's a young man of perception," I said. "Was it he who suggested you ought to be analyzed, once he'd got you interested?"

"I forget. Perhaps it was." Felix was vague. "Listen, what's that?"

I had heard what had caught his attention. Someone was walking about in the flat overhead.

"Perhaps Bob's gone up to do a little more investigating," I suggested.

Felix shook his head. "Not his footsteps. Not nearly heavy enough."

To confirm that, Bob returned to the sitting-room just then. Felix pointed up at the ceiling.

"Someone's got in up there, Bob."

But now there was only silence overhead. Whoever it was

had either stood still or had sat down. Bob frowned slightly, waiting, but as the silence continued, he asked, "Are you sure about it?"

"Positive," Felix answered.

Bob looked questioningly at me.

"Yes," I said.

"I suppose it's the Farrars," he said.

"It sounded like only one person," I said.

"One of them might have come ahead of the other, but perhaps I'd better go up and make sure. Help yourselves to another drink." He went out again.

We both refrained from refilling our glasses. Sitting down, Felix said, "The last thing I'd ever have expected of myself is that I could become friends with a policeman, yet really I've a great regard for Bob, but I see I shall have to explain to him sometime that this isn't the kind of sherry you can offer your guests, even if it's what you like yourself."

"You know he didn't believe your explanation of what we were doing up there, don't you?" I said.

"Probably he didn't."

"So why not tell him the truth, as you know him so well?"

"Because the truth commits one so horribly," Felix said. "You can't get out of it, even when you want to. But as long as there's an element of uncertainty about everything you say, you can always adjust it as you go along. That's what lawyers do, I've been told. Some of their really unintelligible letters are written that way on purpose."

Bob Hazell's firm footsteps were audible overhead, then there was a pause, then we heard them again, accompanied by the lighter footsteps that we had heard earlier. A minute or so passed, then we heard him come in at his own door, which he had left open when he went upstairs, and say something to the person whom he had brought down with him. He opened the sitting-room door and ushered Karen Farrar in ahead of him.

She was dressed exactly as she had been on Saturday evening in the flower-patterned cotton dress she had worn then, and she had sandals on her bare feet, though these looked a little dirtier than they had on Saturday, while the varnish on her toe-nails was cracked. Her long, pale gold hair looked tangled. She was wearing her great silver ring with the dragon's head on it and she moved forward with the drooping kind of grace that I remembered. The main thing about her that was different was that her eyelids were red and swollen and there were tear-stains on her cheeks.

Bob's attitude towards her seemed protective. "Karen needs a drink," he said. "What'll you have, Karen?"

"Brandy, please," she answered without hesitation. Giving Felix and me a vague, puzzled glance, as if she wondered where she had seen us before, she sank down on the brown pseudo-leather sofa, covered her face with her hands and resumed her crying, as uninhibited about it as a child.

It turned out that Bob had no brandy, so he gave her whisky instead.

"Ted's gone, you see," he said.

She lifted up her head and wailed, "Gone! Gone after that bitch Audrey! And they wouldn't have told me a thing about it if I hadn't found his ticket and passport in his pocket. He's gone and left me all alone—oh, God, what am I going to do about it?"

CHAPTER 6

I knew there was something wrong with what she said as soon as she had said it, yet the sight of her, so young, so fragile, so untidy, with the tears streaming down her cheeks, confused me and I could not grasp what it was that was so nearly clear to me.

What I said seemed almost beside the point. "I thought Audrey was going home to marry an Australian."

"Did she tell you so?" Felix asked.

"I'm not sure. Perhaps not. Not actually. But look—" I had got hold of the thought that I had been pursuing. "Audrey left early on Sunday and your husband can't have gone with her, Karen, because he was at home till Sunday evening, wasn't he? Didn't Felix come in to see you and find the two of you there together?"

She sniffed and rubbed at her eyes with the back of her hand, like a five-year-old child.

"Oh yes, he didn't leave with her," she said. "They were going to meet in Singapore. I don't know why they didn't go together, but he told me there was some job he had to do on Sunday, and he wouldn't have told me a thing about leaving me if I hadn't found his ticket and passport. He was just going to disappear and not come back. He was afraid of scenes, you see. He could make awful scenes himself, but he couldn't bear it if anybody else did." She had found her handkerchief by now and mopped her face temporarily dry. "He'd told me he was going to some auction or other in Yorkshire on Monday and might be gone a few days, but while he was out on Sunday morning I started packing a suitcase for him to take away next day, and when I put in his good suit in case he was going to need it, though he didn't often, I felt something in a pocket and there they were, his passport, his ticket and some traveller's cheques. Quite a lot of money. I didn't count how much, but there were a lot of them. So when he came home to lunch on Sunday I asked what on earth these were for and he told me—told me—" She choked. "He told me he was leaving me and joining that woman. Of course, I've always known what she was and it's made me sick to hear everyone saying how good and kind and bloody wonderful she was, and I've always known Ted didn't care for me, but I always thought that was because he'd never got over losing Jill. And I don't think he has, I think she's the only woman he's ever cared about, and this thing with Audrey won't last, but knowing that isn't much help to me now, is it? Because whatever he does, he won't come back to me and I just don't know what I'm going to do!"

"Just a moment, Karen," Bob Hazell said gently. "You say Ted was going to join Audrey in Singapore. Did you notice if his ticket was only to Singapore, or did it go all the way through to Sydney?"

She looked at him blankly. "I don't know. I didn't think. I know it said Singapore."

"And that's all?"

She repeated, "I don't know. I was so puzzled, so—so upset. . . . I mean, all that money in traveller's cheques when we're always so short . . ."

"So you didn't look carefully?"

"I suppose I didn't."

"But he told you he was going to Sydney with Audrey?"

She nodded, beginning to frown as she gazed at him as if she were beginning to feel some puzzling menace in his questions.

"Yes, when he got home," she said. "First Jasper came in

and I told him what I'd found and asked him what he thought it meant, but he didn't seem interested. You know what Jasper's like. He's never really interested in anyone but himself. Even if he thinks he's in love with someone, as he did with Audrey and before that of course with Jill, it's really only himself he's thinking about and watching all the time."

"Narcissism," Felix muttered.

She went on, "And then Ted got home and I was just asking him what the ticket and things were for when the police came and took Jasper away. So it was after that that I asked Ted again why he was going abroad without telling me anything about it, and that's when he told me he was going to join Audrey." She turned to Felix. "And that's when you came in. I'm sorry, I don't think we were very nice to you."

"I knew something was wrong," he said. "I thought you'd been quarrelling, so I didn't stay."

She gave a deep sigh. "It wasn't exactly a quarrel. It was worse than that. It was the end of everything. And now I don't know what to do." She clenched her fists and pounded her knees with them. With suppressed violence, she exclaimed, "I—don't—know—what—to—do!"

"Is money one of your worries?" Felix asked, going quickly to what usually seemed to him the central point in any problem. "Did he leave you anything?"

"Nothing—almost nothing," she said desperately. "He went off in the evening and yesterday I went to the bank to find out what was left in our account and there was just thirty-seven pounds eighty-two pence. And we owe rent for that awful old flat of ours and our landlord's a beast who'd never listen if I tried to explain what had happened and said I'd pay off everything as soon as I could. So I've been sitting in there, keeping out of his way and trying to decide what I ought to do, and at last I thought that if I slipped out with a suitcase when it was dark and came here, he wouldn't know where to find me. We've paid an advance on this flat, so that's all right for the moment. And I could have a little time to think about everything and try to decide what to do."

"How much do you owe the landlord of that other flat?" Felix asked.

"Forty pounds," she said. "It's only for a week and you wouldn't think a dump like that could cost forty pounds, but it did."

Felix glanced at Bob Hazell and me. People's financial troubles always moved him deeply. "I should think we could manage that between us."

Bob and I nodded.

"Oh, I couldn't . . ." she began, then changed her mind and said, "Well, as a loan then, it would help."

"Then there's the shop," Felix went on. "You must have quite a bit of stuff in it that's worth a certain amount."

"But it isn't mine," she said. "It belongs to Ted."

"From the sound of things, he won't be coming back to claim it," Felix said. "I'd regard it as your own."

"But I don't understand anything about the shop," she said. "Ted never wanted me to help with it, so I don't even know how to start getting rid of the things."

"You could put it all into an auction," Felix said. "Jasper may be able to help there, or perhaps Rose Avery. They must both know something about auction rooms and so on. That'll tide you over. And then, I suppose, when you've got your breath, the best thing would be to look for a job. What did you do before you married Ted?"

"I wasn't exactly in a job," she said. "I was living with someone else. An artist. I was his model at first, but I wasn't any good at it, and anyway, it wasn't for very long and I couldn't go back to him for help because he's very successful now and gone to live in the South of France and he wouldn't be interested in me. And before that I was a teacher in an infants' school for a bit, and I quite liked that, but I couldn't manage the discipline. It isn't a thing I understand. And be-

fore that I was one of the girls who take the money in a supermarket, and I always got the money wrong. I could do the
sums in my head, but I couldn't handle that sort of adding
thing they had. And before that—"

"I see, I see," Felix said. "It's obvious you're adaptable, like
me. That ought to make things easier. We'll find you something."

"But I simply can't believe this," I broke in. "I'm sure
Audrey was going home to marry an Australian. And even if
I'm wrong about that, I can't believe she was devious and dis-
honest. If she was going off with your husband, Karen, she
wouldn't have let him deceive you about it right up to the
last minute, having you both here to a party on Saturday and
all."

"Listen to her," Felix said. "She hasn't any understanding
of what people can do."

Karen gave a sombre shake of her head. "She took you all
in. She took me in too till I found out from Ted why he'd got
those tickets and things."

"Well, I'm certain she never dreamt he'd go off leaving you
with only thirty-seven pounds eighty-two pence," I said. "It
simply isn't like her."

"Why not?" she asked. "If you steal someone's husband,
why should you worry about stealing her money too?"

"The two things seem to me somehow different," I said.
"One's emotional, the other's cold-blooded."

"Oh, not necessarily," Felix said. "It's easy to become extremely emotional about money. The trouble with you, Virginia, is that you've never had to worry about it seriously. You
objected to my buying fillet steaks because you said you
couldn't afford them, but really you could and you've always
had enough to get by. Not like this poor girl." He turned back
to Karen. "Did you mean what you said, Karen, that Ted's
never got over losing Jill?"

"Yes, I always knew that," she said. "I knew he'd leave me

sooner or later. People always have. I don't know what it is
about me, because I'm naturally very faithful myself. Even
now, if Ted came back to me, I'd take him back. I know it'd
be stupid and there'd be somebody else soon, still I'd do it.
I'm very easily imposed upon. Several people have told me
so."

"A born victim," Felix said. "I'm one myself, so I understand you. You need someone to look after you. But you'll always choose someone who'll exploit you."

I had never thought of Felix as a born victim. He was too
adroit at victimizing other people. And if he was implying in-
directly that I had exploited him, it was enough to make me
feel very angry. In my view, I was the one who had been
exploited in our marriage. Not financially. Felix might help
himself to relatively small sums from my handbag when he
felt like it, but he could also be generous and he had always
insisted on our having separate bank accounts, I think so that
he could never be tempted to draw unduly on my share of a
joint account. When I had told Audrey that he had no moral
sense, I had not really been fair to him. He had a moral code
of his own. My trouble was that I had never been able to
crack it. By now I believed that the only thing that would
keep him reasonably honest would be if he fell in love with a
very rich woman who would maintain him in comfort and se-
curity which he would think it worth his while to cling to,
particularly now that middle age was making itself felt, and
whom he would repay with genuinely tender affection.

Unfortunately he had never fallen in love with any very
rich woman, perhaps because too few such people had ever
come his way, and he happened to be very responsive to mis-
fortune. There was something rather warmer in his sympathy
with Karen than I felt altogether happy about. I could see
him taking on the role of protector, deluding the poor girl
into believing that he was a strong, responsible man of the
kind who would help her in her troubles and never impose on

her. I was relieved when she decided to return to her flat upstairs for the night and when Bob Hazell saw her up to it, leaving Felix and me to go down to the flat below.

We had bread and cheese and coffee, then sat quietly for a while in the sitting-room. I wanted to go to bed but felt too tired to get up and go there. Felix, lying stretched out on the sofa, seemed either to be thinking deeply or else simply to be lost in a dream which was too agreeable for him to want me to interrupt it.

But at last he said, "That girl's one of the people who doesn't expect much of life, isn't she? The kind of person who's satisfied with very little. I wish I saw how to help her."

"I hope you won't try too hard," I said. "That could be the last straw."

"Now why do you have to say that sort of thing? Actually I might be able to put her in the way of something. . . ." He broke off, still dreamily gazing upwards.

Not liking the sound of this, I watched him uneasily, waiting for him to go on, but whatever was in his mind, he did not pursue it.

Instead he said, "Has it occurred to you, Virginia, that the thing Ted had to do on Sunday, which stopped him leaving with Audrey, might have been murdering Marcus?"

I did not see the point of answering that, because it was certain that he was intent on giving me a little talk on the subject and would do so without any prompting from me. So I went on waiting.

After a moment he continued, "He'd a reason to kill Marcus and a reason to frame Jasper. It's true, supposing he did those things, he waited a good while to get around to it, but making up his mind to disappear abroad may have made him decide to clear up unfinished business before he went. It's something one ought to consider."

"His reason, in both cases, being revenge," I said.

"Yes, it was Marcus who was driving the car when they had

the crash that killed Jill and smashed Ted's foot so badly it had to be amputated. And Jasper had had his affair with Jill before that. Not that I know how far that went or if it worried Ted. At the time he seemed to take it casually and he got married again pretty quickly and he went on being friends with Jasper. But suppose all that was just a way of covering up what he meant to do in the end, the murder of Marcus and getting Jasper arrested for it?"

"But what's Jasper's motive for murdering Marcus supposed to be?"

"The same as Ted's really was. Marcus had killed the woman Jasper loved."

"Well, it's possible."

"But you don't like the idea." He turned his head to look at me.

I was not sure if I did or not. Edmund Farrar seemed to me a man who might be violent, even sadistic, but the thing that I still found it difficult to believe was that there was a love affair between him and Audrey. They did not seem to match up with one another. Yet I knew how easy it is to be wrong about such things.

"If you're right," I said hesitantly, "if he did kill Marcus and frame Jasper, the thing we know he didn't do is murder Miss Pace. Karen said he came home for lunch on Sunday and I don't think she's in the mood to give him a fake alibi. And then Jasper went in to see them and then the police came and then you turned up yourself. So that would mean that your idea that the two murders are connected must be wrong."

"Well, yes, I could be wrong about that, couldn't I? What do you think yourself?"

"That I'm very tired and would like to go to bed," I said. "I'm working tomorrow."

"Go ahead then. I suppose you'll want to get up early." He got up from the sofa. "I'll just collect my pyjamas."

He disappeared into the bedroom, returning after a moment with his pyjamas, sheets and a quilt, which he dropped in a heap on the divan at one end of the room that had been the only bed we had ever been able to offer visitors who stayed the night with us. He kissed me good night rather absently, still absorbed in the problems that we had been discussing, gave me precedence in the bathroom and promised to wake me early. I went into the bedroom, got to bed as quickly as I could and fell asleep almost immediately.

It was the sort of profound sleep from which it is extraordinarily difficult to wake. I had drawn the curtains back before I went to bed and there was daylight in the room when I woke, with everything in it clearly visible, yet there was a confused sense of unreality in my mind at finding myself there at all. It felt at the same time so familiar and so deeply strange. It seemed so natural to be there and yet so abnormal. To make it more bewildering, there was Felix coming into the room with morning tea for me on a little tray, the same tray and the same cup and saucer and small teapot that he had faithfully used throughout the years of our marriage. He had always been better at getting up than I was and had always made tea for me. He had shaved and dressed already and told me that it was seven o'clock.

"Early enough for you?" he asked.

"Fine, thank you," I answered.

"You can get your own breakfast, can't you?" he went on. "I thought I was up in such good time I'd go to the office and catch up on some work. I've a lot of letters to write."

"That mysterious work," I said. "I wish you'd tell me what it is."

"I will sometime, but not now. You're never at your best first thing in the morning and just at the moment I'd like to get off. You'll be able to find everything you want, won't you? It's all where it always used to be."

"Yes, I'll manage. And, Felix . . ."

"Yes?"

"Thank you for your hospitality."

He grinned and gave me one of the quick kisses of the kind to which we rationed ourselves nowadays and left me.

I drank my tea and got up. But I did not make breakfast for myself, because I had decided to drive straight home and have it when I got there. I dressed, packed my case, made the bed and went downstairs. I was just about to open the street door when I heard Bob Hazell call out to me. He was coming down the stairs behind me with a smile on his round, ruddy face.

"You're an early bird," he said.

"I've a job to do," I said. "I've got to get home."

I had opened the door but remained standing in the little hall at the foot of the stairs just outside Miss Pace's flat. Her name, in faded ink, was on a card pinned to the door-frame.

"Not a nice morning," Bob remarked, looking out.

It was not. May, as it so often does, after a week or two of fine weather, had turned almost wintry. Sombre clouds were hurrying across the sky, driven by a chilling wind, and a thin, cold rain was falling.

"Felix not on the move yet?" Bob asked. "Lucky chap, he seems to make his own hours."

"Actually he went out some time ago," I said. I felt an impulse to ask Bob if he knew what Felix did, because it seemed to me he knew a good deal about him. But also I had a feeling that this would be going behind Felix's back in a way that I could not justify to myself, though at the same time I knew that this was only a matter of habit that had lingered on from the past and that I did not owe it to him.

Bob went on, "I suppose you wouldn't feel inclined to tell me what you and Felix were really doing in Audrey's flat yesterday evening."

"But he told you," I said. "There was this little old man—"

He clapped me on the shoulder with a big, muscular hand.

"You aren't a good liar, Virginia. Nor is Felix really, though he thinks he is. He embroiders everything too much. If that little old man hadn't had a hump I might have believed in him, but the hump was just something too much."

"So he wasn't that grass of yours."

He laughed. "You didn't believe that, did you? I could see you didn't."

"I think you're an uncomfortably shrewd man, Bob."

"I work at it." He stood in the doorway, looking out at the rain as if he found the prospect of going out into it very uninviting. "Now if you should feel inclined to tell me what you were really doing . . ." He looked at me questioningly.

It would have been very easy to tell him the truth. There was something about him which made it tempting to talk to him. He had an air of comfortable common sense, of dependability, which made it seem natural to confide in him. But I controlled myself.

"It was nothing really," I said. "Just Felix being inquisitive."

"I see." It was obvious that he did not believe me, but he strode out into the rain and away down the street while I made a dash for my car.

Driving homewards with the windscreen wipers slashing backwards and forwards across my vision and the morning traffic thickening as the rush hour developed, I grew annoyed with myself because of what I had so nearly told Bob. Not that I thought it could have been anything but a good thing for him to know the truth about Miss Pace having seen Jasper on Sunday morning. I could see absolutely nothing against it. But it worried me to think that just because Bob was such a solid, responsible kind of man, the very opposite of Felix to whom I found it so great an effort to be loyal, though I still had the habit of trying, I had been near to telling him everything that Felix had wanted kept a secret.

As I left the suburbs behind and the traffic thinned, I

began to think once more about Felix's occupation and the
letters that he had told me he was going to write that morning. Could they be begging letters? I wondered. He had once
gone through a phase of writing them with a fair amount of
success. One of his friends in the Waggoners had put him up
to it. He had begun by having some letter paper printed with
the name of an imaginary charity, giving an accommodation
address. It had been something to do with disabled children.
Then he had bought a large consignment of very cheap plastic combs and, picking names from directories in various parts
of the country, had sent the present of a comb, along with an
appeal for a contribution to the charity and a stamped
addressed envelope for a reply, to a large number of people. If
they did not wish to contribute, he had always written, they
should simply return the comb, and it was extraordinary how
many people had found it easier to send him a small donation
rather than to do that. The consciences of only a few had allowed them to keep the comb and send no money. He had
claimed that it was the stamped addressed envelope that did
it. Very few people can bring themselves to throw away a
stamp, and to soak it off the envelope and glue it to another is
really too much trouble. So for a little while Felix had done
quite well, but luckily he had grown tired of the ploy before
the police caught up with him. But he could be doing something of the same sort now, I thought. If he was, it was not
surprising that he did not want me to know of it.

Reaching home, I changed out of the dress in which I had
gone to London the evening before, put on the suit that I
usually wore to work, made coffee and toast and was just in
time for my first appointment at the clinic. It was only my
morning that was full up. My afternoon was free. I had had a
vague intention of using it to do some gardening, but also I
had a feeling that perhaps I should call in on Rose Avery to
see how she was, and as the rain kept on and gardening was

out of the question, I cooked myself a chop for lunch, then got back into my car and drove to the Averys' shop.

The blind was down over the window and a notice hanging on the door said, "Closed." But there was a bell beside the door and I rang it. After a little while I heard footsteps inside and Rose opened the door. She did not smile or show any feeling on seeing me, she only gave a little nod of her head as if I had asked her if I might come in and she were agreeing, and held the door further open. Her green, slightly slanting eyes that had always had the look of melancholy that I had never understood and her small puckish face were very tired. She was stooping, too, as if she had suddenly grown old and had not the strength to hold herself upright.

Turning towards a door at the back of the shop through which I had never been taken, she said, "We'll go upstairs. I don't use the office."

The door opened straight on to a steep, narrow staircase which she climbed ahead of me. She took me into a very small sitting-room that overlooked the street. I am not sure what I had expected it to be like. I think I had assumed that in a modest way it would be luxurious, because the Averys' good clothes and their Rover had convinced me that they had at least comfortable means, while from the quality of the goods in their shop I knew that they had taste. What I was not prepared for was that the room should be almost empty and that what there was in it—two easy chairs, a cheap little glass and metal coffee table, a bookcase about half filled with paperbacks, a small table with a plastic top which apparently had been used as a dining-table, but which would have looked more in place in a kitchen, and two painted wooden chairs—were all so old and battered that it seemed probable they had been taken over with the shop from its previous owner, in whose hands it had been that peculiarly revolting secondhand clothes shop.

Standing still in the middle of the room, Rose looked

round, as if she were trying to see the room with my eyes, and remarked, "It's not nice, is it?"

"I thought I'd just look in to see how you were," I said. "If I've hit a bad time I'll go away."

She took no notice of what I had said and only repeated dully, "No, it's not very nice. I never could believe we'd be staying, you see. I thought we'd soon be moving on again. Not quite as soon as I shall be now, but soon, all the same. It never seemed worth while to do anything to the place, but it's horrid, I hate it, I've always hated it. I'll be glad to get away."

She moved to one of the chairs and sat down. I took the other.

"You're going to London, are you?" I said.

"I haven't really decided," she answered. "I'm not quite sure where I'll be allowed to go. Perhaps I won't even manage to get away at all."

"I don't understand," I said. "Who's going to stop you going?"

"I'm not quite sure," she said. "If I were, and if they knew I were, I don't think I'd get anywhere."

There was a sound of dreary defeat in her tone, of hopeless resignation.

I studied her exhausted face and it seemed to me that what showed on it most, strangely enough, was fear.

"It isn't the police you're talking about, is it?" I said. "They aren't trying to stop you going away."

"The police!" she said with contempt in her voice. "All they've done is make life impossible for us ever since we came here, letting us know they were watching us all the time. But they've never been much interested in me, and now that Marcus is dead they'll leave me alone. No, it's the others."

I had a feeling that I was talking to someone who was almost in a hypnotized state and that if I said the wrong thing, shocking her back too abruptly to normal consciousness, I could do her harm.

"The others who killed Marcus?" I said quietly, trying to make it sound a matter-of-fact thing to be asking.

She nodded. "Yes. I always had the feeling they'd do it sooner or later. He wasn't really much use to them any longer."

"But you don't know who they are?"

I was tense, waiting for her to answer, but my question had the effect that I had wanted to avoid, except that there was no sign of it doing her any harm. She blinked several times, focused her eyes on my face and smiled.

"Don't listen to me, Virginia," she said in a more natural tone. "I've been going round in a sort of dream for the last day or two, making up all sorts of nonsense in my head. I see enemies everywhere. Paranoia. All delusions. I've always been inclined that way."

"Marcus's murder wasn't a delusion," I said.

"D'you know, sometimes I feel almost as if it were. The police came and took him away, just as they did the last time, only this time he happens to be dead, that's the only difference. And a lot of the time I find it quite hard to believe in that. Of course you know what I'm talking about, don't you?"

"Not really," I said. "I've a sort of idea, but I could be quite wrong."

"That's funny, I always had the feeling you understood about us." She leant back, folding her hands behind her head. "It was one of the reasons I 'liked you. I thought you'd guessed what we were and that you didn't mind. You knew I didn't tell you the truth about us, didn't you?"

"I think so, yes. But hadn't you better be careful what you tell me now? Don't tell me anything you're going to wish you hadn't."

"What does it matter, now Marcus is dead? I feel like talking. Actually I've told the police everything I know, which isn't much more than they knew already, but talking to a friend is different. I can't think when I did such a thing last. One seems to shed a load, doing it. But perhaps you mind. Is that why you told me to be careful?"

"No, I was thinking of you."

"It could be a mistake to talk, I suppose. We all make mistakes. Marcus's was getting caught and sent to prison. That's what I was going to tell you about, but I felt so sure you knew it. I've almost told you about it once or twice, haven't I?"

"Yes, I realize that," I said. "And I guessed it might be what you just couldn't quite bring yourself to tell me. All the same, I wasn't sure. What had he done?"

"What d'you think?"

"I thought, as he was in the antique trade, he might have been receiving stolen property."

She gave an abrupt laugh with a very hard edge to it. "If it were only that! No, no, it was drugs. Pushing drugs. Heroin. Very serious." Her gaze on me sharpened. "Doesn't that horrify you? Pushing death and destruction on the stupid and the helpless. A nice woman like you ought to be revolted."

I answered slowly, "I suppose I am. Did you know about it?"

"Not at first. Not when we got married. But Marcus had already built up quite a good little connection in that school he taught in and among the art students in the school where he was trained, and after a little while I noticed we always had more money than I could account for and I challenged him about it. At first he tried the old chestnut on me, saying he'd won it gambling, but every so often he used to have attacks of conscience and break down and cry and say he couldn't go on, only they'd never let him go. 'They.' He meant the people who supplied him. And soon I had the whole story, or most of it, out of him. The one thing he'd never tell me was who 'they' were. He said it was safer for me not to know."

"Do you know it now?"

"No."

It was said positively, but during the time that I had known her my ear had become tuned in to when Rose was not telling the truth and I had my doubts of it now.

"What did you do?" I asked.

"Oh, I took a very high line," she said. "I told him he'd got to give the thing up and that he'd have to pluck up his courage to tell his contacts, whoever they were, that he couldn't go on any longer, and that he must get right away from the school and all his old customers and we'd set up somewhere new, doing something new. And he agreed and we borrowed money and went down to Bristol and opened a little antique shop there. It seemed to work splendidly for a time, but then the old trouble began again—that we'd too much money—and I realized that it wasn't to buy antiques that a good many of our customers came into the shop. And then one day the police arrived and took him away. He got two years."

"What did you do while he was in prison?" I asked.

"I sold up our stock and went back to London and got a job as a secretary again. I'd made up my mind to break off with him, but then one day near the end of his sentence— he'd got time off for good behaviour—Roland appeared and, well, he persuaded me I was Marcus's only hope and that if I gave him up he'd go to pieces completely. Prison, Roland said, had really broken him. So I agreed to try again."

"It's Mr. Straker you mean."

"Yes."

"How did he come on the scene?"

She took a moment to reply, considering, I thought, how much to tell me. Then she went on with a sound of reluctance. "You know him. He's a very rich man and he's always gone in for good works in a big way. He doesn't seem to have any other idea of how to spend his money. One of his things was a committee concerned with the rehabilitation of ex-convicts. He got to know Marcus when he was in prison and thought he could sort him out if he had a chance. So, as I said, he came to see me and I agreed to make another effort. He promised to help us if I would, and he did. When Marcus came out nearly two years ago he lent us money and then, when the old woman who ran the secondhand clothes shop here decided to retire and the shop became available, he let us know about it and we took it over and moved in. And it's done better than I expected, but all the same . . ." She paused for some time, passing a hand wearily across her forehead. "All the same, it wouldn't have paid for the Rover that Marcus had delivered to us one day, or explain how he got the money to buy me some good clothes. But I was tired of asking him where the money came from, so I took it and bought the clothes and I drove the Rover. Marcus couldn't drive it himself after he had his licence suspended after a smash he was in with the Farrars. I got to know the Farrars first when we were in Bristol. They were very good to me all the time Marcus was in prison, specially Jill. I've missed her very much since she died. Marcus knew Ted a long time before. They were at the same art school together."

She repeated the gesture of passing a hand across her forehead and looked round the room.

"God, how I hate this place!" she said. "I've never felt it was home. I knew we couldn't stay here. That's why I never bothered with it and why I never brought you up here. Of course the police knew all about us from the first and were keeping an eye on us and they'd have got Marcus again sometime soon if he hadn't been killed. And sometimes I almost hoped they would, because one of the things I couldn't bear was that Roland was always our best customer, which was only to help us, but he kept coming here to buy things and Marcus used to laugh about it and call him a fool and make a point of overcharging him, and Roland knew it and let him. There was something horribly humiliating about it. All right,

I know he's in love with me, but that wasn't why he did it. He did it because he's a really good man."

"Are you sure of that?" I asked.

She started, as if she had half forgotten that she was talking to me and not only to herself.

"Of course I'm sure," she said. "What made you ask?"

I was not sure myself and began to wish that I had not done so. I said uncertainly, "I only wondered if it was possible that Marcus had some hold on him and that's why he was helping you."

"I don't understand you." Then her gaze sharpened again. "Are you talking about *blackmail?*"

"Well, is it possible that this time Marcus's money wasn't coming from pushing drugs after all? I believe prison's a good place for picking up secrets. If Marcus had found out something about Mr. Straker while he was in there, something he could use against him, something to do with how he became so rich—"

"Stop!" she shouted. She clutched her temples with both hands. "Didn't I tell you Roland's a really good man? He's never in his life done anything he could be blackmailed for. He's much too good for me. I've known for months Marcus had gone back to the drugs game and I just sat back and let him. I was too tired of everything to stop him. But I won't let you say horrible things about Roland. You'll be saying next he murdered Marcus because he was being blackmailed by him, or because he wanted me, but he didn't, he didn't! I tell you, he's a really good man, the only one I've ever known, and I'd love him if he weren't so much too good for me. Now, for God's sake, go and leave me alone! I'm used to being alone. I like it. It's better than all this talking. I don't need anybody. Why don't you go?" Tears had started to run down her cheeks and her voice had risen almost to a shriek.

I did not know what else to do, so I did as she asked and got up and left her.

CHAPTER 7

If Rose had been less vehement, I should have felt more convinced. I did not know what it was about her, but I always found it difficult to believe the whole of what she told me. Perhaps Roland Straker was as good a man as she had said, but perhaps he was not. I had no reason to think that he was not and I had never felt any doubt of him before, but as I drove home I began to worry over what kind of man he really was.

I guessed that what had just started me wondering about him was the feeling that Rose herself was scared that he might not be all he seemed. It could even be that she knew he was not and that the fear I had felt behind her sudden outburst was that this might be discovered. But did that mean that I was seriously considering the possibility that he could be involved in pushing drugs, that that was where his money came from, that he might even be Marcus's murderer?

No, I told myself, of course not. That was sheer fantasy of the kind that might have attracted Felix but was really not my line. Normally I am fairly sober in my assessment of people and I remembered how much I had liked Roland Straker when he was my patient. On the whole, I reflected, it would be sensible at the present moment to rely on first impressions and not start thinking of a nice man as if he might be an ogre. All the same, I was deeply upset by the discovery that drugs had come into the picture. I knew very little about them, but thought of everything to do with the enormous profits to be made out of their secret distribution with a horror that was more or less in the same class as my feelings about cold-blooded terrorism.

As I turned into Ellsworthy Street I saw that there was a car at my gate and that the car was a Rolls. I knew only one person who possessed a Rolls and that was Roland Straker. I could not think why he should have come to call on me, and in the mood I was in I did not look forward to seeing him, but it was not to be avoided. When I stopped my car behind his, I saw him standing in my porch. It looked as if he had only just arrived and rung my bell and was now waiting for an answer.

I left my car in the road instead of putting it into the garage and went up the path to the door. He turned when he heard my footsteps.

"Ah, I'm so glad I've caught you," he said. "May I come in? I'd like to talk to you."

I unlocked the door and let him in.

"How are you?" I asked. "Not more of the old trouble with your hip, I hope."

"Oh no, this isn't a professional visit."

I had known that it was not, since if it had been the appointment would have been made through the usual medical channels, but it had been something to say.

"Will you have some tea?" I asked as he limped after me into the sitting-room. Why was it that his limp and the thought of drugs were somehow connected in my mind? "I could get it in a minute."

"Oh no—no, thank you—please don't trouble. I just wanted to ask a favour of you." He went to the end of the room and stood looking out at the garden. The lilacs were beginning to fade and in the last day or two their soft purples had acquired a tarnished look which foretold the end of the spring, while the few rosebuds that were beginning to open heralded the summer, but in the steady rain it all had a depressing air. However, he went on, "You've a very charming place here."

I thought of his mansion on the edge of the town with its lofty rooms and its park-like grounds.

"At least it's very little trouble to look after," I said.

"Do you do it all yourself?"

"I've a nice woman who comes in twice a week and does the house for me, but I manage the garden."

"And you do your job too. I think you're someone who manages to keep her whole life uncommonly well organized."

"I've never thought so myself," I said. "I've made some quite serious blunders in my time."

"Haven't we all?" He turned and regarded me along the length of the roof with the singular calm that I had noticed before in the grey eyes under his heavy dark eyebrows. "I'm afraid I made one serious blunder not so very long ago and someone I care for very deeply is paying for it."

I had sat down and gestured to him to take the chair facing me across the empty fireplace, but he remained where he was with his back to the window.

"I want to talk to you about Rose Avery," he said. "Would it be too much to ask you to befriend her? She needs someone like you."

I smiled in a way that I imagine was more than a little wry. "I don't think she'd agree with you. Actually I've just been to see her and was asked by her to leave. No, not asked. I was ordered out."

There was no need, I thought, to mention the fact that it was what I had said about him that had provoked this.

"All the same, she needs a friend," he said. "She's a very lonely person."

"I know that."

"I'm doing what I can for her, but I feel it's another woman she needs. I can't help showing her my feelings and at the moment she only finds that an embarrassment. In time I want to ask her to marry me and she knows it and it's making her keep me at arm's length. Of course, I shouldn't think of doing such a thing at a time like this and probably she knows that too, yet the thought of it disturbs her. I believe she cares for me, but at present she's frightened of letting herself feel anything. I have to be very careful when I'm with her and I know she doesn't talk openly to me in the way she needs. But with you it would be different."

There was a curious formality in the way he spoke, yet at the same time a quiet candour that was very appealing. I wondered how I could ever have had any suspicions of him.

"She talked quite openly to me today," I said, "and then she regretted it. I don't know that I'll ever be able to help her much."

"But perhaps you could try."

I met his calm gaze thoughtfully. "Exactly what is it you want me to do, Mr. Straker?"

"Oh, I leave that to you. Just be there if she wants you."

"Of course I'll do that."

"And don't believe any evil of her. Some people may do so."

"Those being the police?"

He walked forward at last and took the chair facing me.

"So she talked to you a good deal today," he said, "and you know something of what she's been through."

"I know Marcus was in prison for peddling drugs and she stuck to him through it. I know you helped them when he came out and I know she thought he'd gone back to doing it."

"Did she tell you it was I who persuaded her to stick to him when she was thinking of breaking off with him?"

"Yes."

"That was the blunder I made that I spoke of just now. I'd no right to do it. But I didn't know her yet, I was only thinking of Marcus, and probably seeing myself as a very fine and splendid character who was quite infallible about right and wrong. I'm not saying this now because as I got to know her better I fell in love with her. If Marcus had not turned out to be beyond redemption I believe it would have been best for her to stick to him and I should never have let her know my feelings. But I had no right to interfere in her life in the way I did."

"When did you find out Marcus had gone back to pushing drugs?"

"I'm not sure how long ago it was. Rose told me she was afraid of it and I spoke to Marcus about it and he denied it absolutely. That didn't necessarily mean anything. He'd naturally deny it. But I can't say I'd any definite evidence of it, though since his murder I've assumed Rose was right."

"You think his murder was connected with those activities?"

"Isn't that probable? Indeed, almost certain?"

"But what had he done to make murder necessary? If he was simply handling the sale of drugs in this area, why should he have to be got rid of?"

"There's an obvious answer to that. That he was passing on information."

"To the police?"

"Probably. They'd had him under observation ever since he came here and they may have promised him some degree of immunity if he helped them."

"There's just one thing about that explanation that I don't like," I said.

"What's that?"

"The silver bracelet that was found under his body. Where did these drug smugglers who were running the operation get hold of it?"

He considered it, nodded and said, "Yes, I should have thought of that. Where do you think it came from?"

"It must have come from someone who got the bracelet from Jasper Noble, or from someone like the Averys themselves, who had his things on sale. And for some reason this person wanted to incriminate Jasper, either because he had something against him or because he was a useful sort of scapegoat, and there's only one person I know of whom that fits and that's Edmund Farrar."

"Ah yes, the man whose wife was killed in the accident and who lost his foot when Marcus was driving. Had he anything special against Jasper?"

"I've been told Jasper was in love with Edmund Farrar's wife. I don't know if she responded, but perhaps she did."

"I see. But have you thought that it may have been Noble himself who left the bracelet there after it got broken in the struggle that seems to have taken place, that he wasn't framed by someone else? If he was connected with the drug business too and believed that Marcus was handing on information about it to the police, that would give him a motive quite apart from anything to do with that accident. And it seems probable that whoever it was knew the Averys fairly well, because he was aware that Rose went to church on Sundays and that she'd be out in the morning. It's true she was still in the house when he arrived and she overheard part of the quarrel, but if she'd gone in and found him, he might simply have called the murder off for the time being. Alternatively, she might have been a victim too."

"But Jasper had an—" With annoyance at myself for what I had nearly said, I stopped. I remembered that officially Jasper had no alibi. I did not know why both he and Felix wanted it kept secret, but Jasper himself had said to Roland Straker and the others of us who had been with him the evening before in the Rose and Crown that he had spent Sunday morning at home in bed.

Perhaps fortunately, Mr. Straker misunderstood me. "Yes, yes, he has an undamaged bracelet that he was wearing when he was arrested. But no doubt he had any number of them. I'm surprised at the police taking it seriously enough to let him go just on that account. I'm inclined to believe there must have been other reasons. But to return to Rose, Mrs. Freer, will you help her if she needs you? May I tell her she can rely on you?"

"I'll do anything I can," I said, though I was a little puzzled by my own reluctance to say it. I felt as if I were being pushed into a corner from which I might not be able to escape. "But will you tell me one thing, Mr. Straker?"

"Yes?"

"Do the police know you knew Marcus had gone back to selling drugs?"

For a moment I thought I saw someone looking at me through those calm grey eyes who was quite different from anyone I had ever had a glimpse of before, someone both angry and wary. However, it was only for an instant. Almost immediately they were the eyes I knew.

"You think they ought to know?" he asked.

"Oh, not necessarily. I just want to know where I am," I said.

"I've put myself in your hands," he said. "I've told you about my feelings for Rose and I expect you can understand that my silence from the first was dictated simply by what I thought would help her most. And in fact all she had were suspicions, together with some knowledge of Marcus's character. I believe he was selling drugs quite recently, but I've no evidence of it. Does that satisfy you?"

It sounded to me like a quibble, but I honestly wanted to help Rose, if she would let me do it, though I still had a strange uneasiness at committing myself to it in words that would be hard to withdraw.

"She couldn't have been made to give evidence against her husband, could she?" I said. "So unless there's some proof that she was involved herself with what Marcus was doing she can't get into trouble."

"I believe that's true." Roland Straker got to his feet, a tall, well-built man of sixty, a little old to be passionately in love, though evidently not beyond it. "And I believe I can count on you to do what you can for her. Thank you, in any case, for listening to me. By the way, have you any news of our dear Audrey Beasley? I'll never forget what a wonderful nurse that girl was. Why aren't there more like her?"

"I believe she's back in Australia by now," I said.

"Ah yes, getting married. I wish I knew when. I'd send her a wedding present. When did she leave?"

"On Sunday."

"So she'll certainly have reached Sydney."

Unless, I thought, she had her reasons for lingering in Singapore. But I still resisted the thought of that though the evidence of it seemed clear enough.

"Yes, of course," I said.

He thanked me again for listening to him, then he left.

As the Rolls drove away I went to the kitchen and made myself the tea that he had refused. I did not often bother with tea in the afternoon, but I was in a state of uncomfortable tension and it still seemed early for a drink. I am conventional about that. I find it very difficult to drink out of hours. So I made tea and carried the tray into the sitting-room and as I drank tried to think out what was worrying me about the interview I had just had, an interview with a man whom I had always liked and trusted.

That one glance he had given me when his personality seemed to change had been disturbing, yet in someone who in his own field undoubtedly wielded a good deal of power and was not used to being thwarted, there was nothing really surprising about it. And it had come and gone so swiftly that perhaps I had imagined it. No, it was something else that nagged at my mind.

I had got to my third cup of tea before I was sure of what it was. It was simply that I did not feel certain that in my interview with Rose she had not been trying to use me. She had given me a version of her relationship with Marcus that was sure to gain my sympathy, portraying herself as the loyal, long-suffering wife of a wicked man whom to the end she had been trying to help, and yet I felt no certainty that she had not shared in his wickedness. And if in fact that was true and she had been in his drug trading with him, what did that make Roland Straker, her dupe or her accomplice?

I was startled at myself when I arrived at that point, because I do not believe that I am naturally a suspicious person. My inclination now was to brush my suspicions aside, to believe Rose and to believe Roland Straker, and actually I thought that it would be easier to do this now that my doubts had become explicit and were not merely a foggy uncertainty at the back of my mind. But knowing Felix for as long as I had, having been married to him for a time and having gone on seeing a fair amount of him even after that had broken up, had made an alteration in my nature to which I had never quite become accustomed. I found it extraordinarily difficult to take people on trust.

This sometimes made me very unhappy, because I have always found it much less effort to accept people as what they seem to be than to peer doubtingly into the dark places in their characters. But if I had been twisted so that I could not help doing this, there was nothing much that I could do about it. Meanwhile, I had had an idea of something that it might be useful to do. I took the tea-tray out to the kitchen, then came back to the telephone and dialled Tim Dancey's number in Jellingham.

I knew that the chances were that he was still at the hospital and that there would be no answer, in which case I would have to try again later, but when the telephone had rung only three or four times it was picked up and I heard him say, "Dancey speaking."

"It's Virginia, Tim," I said. "Have you any time to spare? I'd like to talk to you."

"Now, d'you mean?" he asked.

"The sooner the better."

"Unluckily I'm on call tonight," he said, "but I could come round now for a little while. Is that any use?"

"Yes, of course. It won't take long."

"Then I'll be along in about half an hour." He paused. "Is there something wrong, Virginia?"

"I don't know," I said. "I don't really think so. But perhaps . . . No, it can wait till you get here. It would be a bit complicated to explain on the telephone."

"Right. I'll come straight away."

"Thank you, Tim."

He rang off.

As I put my telephone down I began to wonder why I had done what I had. It had not been in our relationship so far for me to turn to him for advice, yet when I had thought of it, it seemed a good idea. As perhaps it was. At least it could do no harm.

I filled some of the time that I had to wait for him by going upstairs, combing my hair and putting on fresh makeup, then came downstairs and put out drinks and glasses in the sitting-room. I no longer felt that it was too early for a drink and nearly always it was over drinks that Tim and I had talked. He arrived in a little less than the half hour that he had promised and with a look of concern in his eyes which could look so oddly old and experienced in a face that was otherwise so young-looking for his age.

"Something *is* wrong," he said, regarding me as I handed him the whisky and water that was his usual drink. "What is it? Felix?"

"For once, no," I answered.

We sat down in the chairs facing each other across the fireplace, where Roland Straker and I had been sitting a little while before.

"Tim, you've been in this part of the world for some time," I said. "What do you know about Roland Straker?"

He gave me a look of astonishment. "Now that's something I was not expecting you to ask me," he said. "What's he done to upset you?"

"Nothing. Nothing at all."

"But you *are* upset."

"I'm puzzled, that's all. He came here to see me this afternoon and he made a quite normal sort of request—I mean, it seems to me normal in the circumstances—but now I'm haunted by the feeling that there may be more behind it than I realized. I'm probably quite wrong, but all the same I thought I'd like to know more about the sort of man he is and I know you've had some contact with him."

"Not very much and what I've had has been mostly official. We've met on the odd committee and so on." He sipped his drink, watching me thoughtfully. "What was the request?"

"Only that I should be as friendly as I can to Rose Avery."

"Rose Avery—she's the widow of the man who was murdered in Allingford a few days ago, is that it?"

"Yes."

"And she's a friend of yours, I think you told me."

"I think I probably told you that I knew her, though not really well."

"And the trouble is, you don't much like her, you're just sorry for her, and you're worried at being asked to befriend her."

"No, it isn't like that at all. Tim, how much do you know about the murder?"

"Not very much, I'm afraid. Just what I've read in the paper. And to tell the truth, I haven't paid much attention to it. I don't often read much about murders. But I'm sorry I didn't this time, since you're involved in it. Go on and tell me something about it."

I was beginning to regret having asked for his help, because I had forgotten how little he knew of the Averys and that there was no reason to expect that he should have taken any special interest in Marcus's murder.

"I suppose I ought to start at the beginning," I said, "but have you time to listen to a rather long story?"

He smiled. "Go on."

"It isn't urgent. Another time would do."

"Let's forget about that, shall we? Let's get on with the story."

"To tell you a little more about the Averys themselves then," I said, "they ran a small sort of antique shop in St. Christopher's Lane. They've been there for about eighteen months and I've bought oddments from them from time to time and I got quite friendly with them. But I always had a queer feeling that they weren't quite what they seemed—I won't bother you with the details of why I felt that—and when Rose told me she'd been a secretary and Marcus had been an art teacher in a comprehensive school I didn't quite believe it. Well, it turns out that what she told me was more or less true, but that there was an interval between the time they gave that up and the time they came here, and Marcus spent a good deal of that time in prison for peddling drugs."

Tim gave a low whistle. "I begin to understand your problem. How far was Rose involved and do you feel you can befriend someone who was? An awkward sort of problem. But how on earth did you find this out?"

"Rose told me herself this afternoon."

"That she and her husband had been peddling drugs? Isn't that rather astonishing?"

"No, she told me it was he who'd been doing it and that she'd tried to stop him."

"Ah, one of those loyal wives. Do you believe her?"

"That's something I'm not sure of."

"I wouldn't if I were you."

"Why not?"

"Well, if it's true that you and she aren't really intimate

friends, she seems to have taken you into her confidence
rather fully and the only reason I can think of why she should
do that is that she wants to get the idea of her innocence
across to you before you've time to doubt her. Then you'd be
on her side if the police get troublesome."

"I've thought of that. At the same time, I think she was
desperate to confide in someone, though I felt she regretted
doing it almost immediately. You see, if what she told me is
true, she's kept her troubles bottled up for years and never
discussed them with anyone. With anyone, that's to say, except Roland Straker."

"Ah, so that's where he comes in. Go on."

But at that moment the telephone began to ring.

I went to answer it. When I said, "Oh yes, Felix," Tim got
to his feet and indicated that he would leave the room so that
I could talk to Felix in private. But I gestured to him to stay
where he was, though I felt a little apprehensive about what
might follow. Conversations with Felix might lead anywhere
and the faint smile on Tim's face as he subsided into his chair
made me feel self-conscious. He and I had often talked about
Felix, but he had never seen me trying to cope with him.

"Virginia, a perfectly extraordinary thing has happened,"
Felix said. "Did you listen to the one o'clock news?"

"No," I said.

"There was an item on it, just a short one, that would have
interested you. A man was arrested at Heathrow this morning, trying to smuggle thousands of pounds' worth of high-
grade heroin into the country from Singapore inside a plastic
artificial foot."

"No!" I said, but this time it was not a negative, it was simply astonishment.

"It didn't give his name, of course, it only said a man was
helping the police with their inquiries—isn't that a bloody
silly formula? I believe the police themselves think it is and
say it was the press and not themselves who thought it up.

Anyway, even before the police turned up here, which they did this afternoon, I took for granted it was Ted Farrar. I don't know how many men with artificial feet travel home from Singapore per day, but I thought it would be a bit too much of a coincidence if there was more than one."

"But when we last heard of Ted he was going *to* Singapore," I said, "not coming back from it."

"Yes, and that explains a good deal, doesn't it?" Felix said. "He didn't go there to meet Audrey. It had nothing to do with her. He only told Karen that that was what he was doing because she found his ticket. Very careless of him to leave it where she could find it. If she hadn't and he'd been gone a few days, she'd have taken for granted he was in Yorkshire, scouring the country for antiques, but as she found the ticket and the passport he had to explain them somehow, so he came up with this story about joining Audrey as a way of getting her off the scent of the heroin. If he hadn't been arrested on his way home he'd have turned up here with deep apologies for any distress he's caused her, and saying he'd realized as soon as he left that he was making a terrible mistake and that he'd turned straight home again as soon as he got to Singapore and hoped she'd take him back."

"And you think she would have?"

"Didn't you hear her say she would?"

"Yes, but people don't always mean what they say. She's been seen by the police, has she, since they arrested him?"

"Yes, they came and searched the flat and put her through some pretty tough questioning, and they searched the Farrars' old flat too, and the shop, but I don't think they found anything."

"Do you think it's possible she knew about the smuggling all the time and told us that story about his having taken off with Audrey by agreement with him, in case anybody wanted to know where he'd vanished to all of a sudden?"

There was a slight pause, then Felix said, "Virginia, you're becoming distinctly peculiar. You doubt everything everybody says. You should be careful. It might develop into some quite serious form of neurosis."

"Let's keep off the psycho-analysis," I said. "I've a feeling you may not have a really good grasp of the subject."

"I suppose you doubt all this I've been telling you," he said.

"No, I don't," I answered. "It would be so easy to check. I'm sure Ted Farrar has been arrested for smuggling heroin, just as you say. I only wonder if Karen is as ignorant as she seems."

"Let me tell you, she's a sweet, sensitive girl," he said indignantly, "who's going through the worst thing that's ever happened to her in her life. What she needs at the moment is understanding and sympathy, not cold-hearted scepticism. She's had enough of that from the police. She's stood up to it with remarkable strength of mind, but all the same she's suffering acutely."

"Are you falling for her?" I asked.

I heard a sound behind me that might have been a chuckle, but I did not look round.

"That's beside the point," Felix said. "And even if I were, and I don't say I am, she can't think of anything now but Ted's troubles. But d'you know something that seems to me rather strange, Virginia?"

"What?"

"You don't seem much surprised at what I told you about Ted trying to bring heroin into the country inside his artificial foot. I'd have expected you to be amazed, as I was, but you seem to take it for granted."

"Well, things have been happening here this afternoon, things Rose has told me. . . ." I hesitated, not wanting to become involved in a long explanation, partly because it seemed a difficult thing to do on the telephone and partly because I thought Tim might not be able to stay much longer and I had hardly got around to what I wanted to ask him. I chose my words with some care, meaning to keep them brief. "Rose told me Marcus had been peddling drugs on and off ever since she knew him and that we were quite right when we guessed he might have been in gaol. Only she said she didn't know who his supplier was. But what you've told me suggests it was probably Ted Farrar. And he may have been the murderer too. Do you remember, we were saying that the police usually get people on information received? Well, I've heard it suggested today that Marcus, after his time in gaol, had actually gone over to the other side and was handing on information to the police and that perhaps that was why he was murdered. There's something that supports that. Rose says that she heard Marcus shouting at someone in their office before she set off for church and it seems to me that if his murderer was accusing him of being an informant he might have been shouting that it wasn't true. That's a bit of a guess, but it's possible, isn't it?"

There was silence on the telephone. I waited, but when I still heard nothing I at last said, "Felix?"

"Yes, I'm here," he said. "I was just thinking. . . . You know, I've had a feeling from the first that there was too much sex in the way we were looking at things. Now it's obvious that was quite right."

"Sex?" I said. "I can't say I've noticed it much."

"What I meant was that we've been thinking of the motive for Marcus's murder as being connected with the death of Jill Farrar," he said. "In other words that the murderer was almost certainly Ted or Jasper. But if it's really to do with smuggling heroin—"

"Just a minute, Felix," I interrupted. The sound of a movement behind me told me that Tim had stood up and I was afraid that he would be quietly slipping out in another moment if I did not stop Felix. "Can I ring you back later and go on with this then? I've an appointment and I ought to rush off."

"Yes—yes, of course," Felix said. "But there's something I've just thought of. . . . Virginia, you know how I've been asking you to tell nobody about what Lilian Pace told me?"

"About her having seen Jasper on Sunday morning?"

"Yes. Well, I think I've been a fool. An awful fool. Of course I oughtn't to have kept quiet about that. And I shouldn't have asked you to do it either. D'you mind changing now and telling everyone you meet who has any connection with the affair about her seeing him?"

"I don't understand."

"Never mind. Will you do it?"

"Tell everyone what Miss Pace told you?"

"Yes."

"Felix, I don't think I like the sound of this," I said.

"Why not?"

"It doesn't sound like you. You were so sure you had good reasons for not talking about it."

"I've got good reasons now for what I'm saying. Anyway, please do it. Tell Rose. Tell anyone who's connected with her."

"I see."

"You will?"

"I suppose so. Good-bye."

"Good-bye." He rang off.

I stood still for a moment, gazing in front of me with my hand still on the telephone, trying to make sense of what Felix had said. It was as if something that I had said had brought about this sudden change in him. After a moment I heard another quiet laugh from Tim.

"I ought to tell you, I heard most of that," he said. "His voice was very clear. And for the first time I felt a certain sympathy with Felix. When you're talking to him your voice changes, do you know that? You turn into a very formidable lady. But tell me something. This man Farrar who was trying to smuggle heroin into the country inside an artificial foot— that *is* what I heard, isn't it?"

"Yes."

"It's an extraordinary thing, but I think I did that amputation. The crash in which his foot got crushed and his wife was killed happened quite near here. I can't remember much about him. I just did a straightforward job. There weren't any complications. It didn't occur to me I was fitting a man with a splendid receptacle for carrying drugs. But what's this about Felix having been told something on Sunday morning that's so important?"

Since Felix had removed his prohibition on my talking about it, I told Tim how Lilian Pace had seen Jasper come down from Audrey's flat and had told Felix about it.

At the end of it Tim was frowning. He said, "Is Felix a fool?"

"It depends what you mean by a fool," I said.

"The question is, is he a fool or a very shrewd operator?"

"Mightn't one be both?"

"I suppose it's possible. Well, to go back to Roland Straker, because that's what you wanted to talk to me about, isn't it? And I really mustn't stay much longer."

I returned to my chair. "I told you he came here to ask me to befriend Rose Avery, and he told me he was in love with her and wanted her to marry him. And a little while before that Rose told me she knew that and thought she might love him if he wasn't much too good for her. And she told me how he'd come to see her when Marcus was in prison and how he persuaded her to stick to him and lent them money when Marcus came out and found the shop they've been running here in Allingford. But the shop obviously wasn't paying and in fact it appears Marcus had gone back to pushing drugs and Rose guessed it and told Mr. Straker about it. So he's known about it for some time and done nothing about it, and that's

understandable if he's very much in love with her. He'd want
to do all he could to protect her. But if it isn't true . . ."

I made a gesture with one hand, hoping that he would fill
in the rest of the sentence.

"If it isn't true," he said, "then he could be the man
behind Marcus. The man behind Farrar. Somewhere in these
operations, I imagine, there has to be money. Money, at least,
must be going somewhere, and Straker certainly seems to
have plenty and I couldn't tell you where it comes from. So
far as I've thought about it at all, which isn't much, I've assumed it was inherited. I believe his family were manufac-
turing people in the North who left him more than he knew
what to do with, and because he's got simple tastes and has a
good deal of the Quaker about him, he's been spending it all
on charity. That's really all I know about him. D'you think
he's a little too good to be true?"

"I can't help wondering."

"But there are good people to be met with occasionally."

"Oh yes."

"I'm sorry I can't help you more."

"It doesn't matter. I expect he's just what he seems to be
and I'm the one who's got warped."

He bent down and kissed me on the cheek. "I'd better go
now. But I'll think about the whole thing. Perhaps I can find
someone who knows more about him than I do. If I put an
ear to the ground I might find out if there are any peculiar
rumours about him floating around. Good-bye."

I did not get up and he let himself out.

After he had gone I sat where I was for some time, trying
to make sense of Felix's change of attitude. Why did he want
me to tell as many people as possible about Lilian Pace having seen Jasper on Sunday morning and having been able to
give him an alibi for Marcus's murder, when only a short
while ago Felix had appeared genuinely scared that this might
be discovered? I wondered if he knew what he was up to, be-

cause now that I knew that there were drug smugglers, in other words, professional criminals, involved in the case, I felt far more frightened myself than I had before. But I could not make any sense of it. However, after I had brooded over it for some time I thought I might as well start doing what he wanted. Going to the telephone again, I picked it up and dialled Rose's number.

CHAPTER 8

As soon as she heard my voice she burst out, "Virginia, I'm sorry—I want to say how sorry I am I spoke to you as I did. It was unforgivable. I don't know how to explain it, except that I know I'm not myself at the moment. I'm truly sorry. You're the only friend I've got here, unless you count Roland, and that's different, and I said those awful things to you. I don't know what came over me, but please try to forget I said any of it. I never meant to drive you away."

"That's all right," I said. "I know the strain you're under. I expect I'd do the same in the circumstances. Tell me, Rose, have you heard about Edmund Farrar's arrest?"

"No," she said. "No, I haven't heard a word. Do you mean it's for Marcus's murder? Are you sure? Why haven't the police told me about it?"

"Actually it was for trying to smuggle heroin into the country inside his artificial foot," I answered.

She was silent for a moment, then said, "*Into* the country? Where's he been?"

"To Singapore," I said. "He was arrested at Heathrow on his way back."

She paused again, then observed thoughtfully, "Ted Farrar. I ought to have known it."

"That he was Marcus's supplier?"

"Yes, and more than that. The brains behind the thing. He always had tremendous influence on Marcus. Sometimes it puzzled me. You're sure about his arrest?"

"It's what Felix told me. He said it was on the one o'clock

news and that the police have been questioning Karen. I
don't think there's any mistake about it."

I heard her give a brief sigh. "I ought to be glad, oughtn't
I?"

"I think I should be, if I were you," I said.

"Yes, I'm going to feel safer now. You know, ever since
Marcus was killed, I've been wondering if I'd be next. I've
been thinking that perhaps Marcus was killed because they
thought he was an informer, so why shouldn't they do the
same to me? They could so easily have believed I knew far
more than I did."

"Did you never suspect Ted of being involved in the
thing?"

"Sometimes I wondered. But I told you he and Jill were
very good to me when Marcus was in prison, so I didn't want
to think anything bad about them."

"Are you sure Ted was the brains at the back of it? You
don't think there was anyone else behind him?"

"I'm not sure about anything. There may have been lots of
people in it. I should think there probably were. In which
case my idea that I'm safer now that they've got Ted is rather
stupid."

"Rose, what do you think about Jasper Noble?" At last I
had got round to what had made me ring her up, in accor-
dance with my promise to Felix. "Do you think he's in with
Marcus and Ted?"

She sounded indifferent. "I suppose it's possible."

"But you aren't sure?"

"I told you, I'm not sure of anything. Why?"

"Only that he did a rather peculiar thing and I wondered if
it fits in somehow. On Sunday morning, round about the
time Marcus was killed, Jasper was seen coming down the
stairs in Little Carbery Street by a woman called Lilian Pace,
who lived on the ground floor. So when Jasper was arrested
because the police found the bracelet under Marcus's body,

he could have told them straight away that she could give him an alibi. Yet he didn't. He seems to have told them, as he told us, that he spent the morning at home."

"How do you know this?"

"Miss Pace told Felix about seeing Jasper."

"Why didn't she tell the police about it when she heard Jasper needed an alibi?"

"Because she was found murdered herself that afternoon. Someone got into her flat and choked her to death."

"Oh, God!" I heard Rose give a hiss of horror. Then after a moment she went on, "But I don't see how that can tie in with Marcus's murder. Why do you think it might?"

"It's just a sort of feeling I have, because of Jasper knowing Ted and Marcus, and the two murders happening on the same day. But I suppose that could be coincidence."

"I should think it must be. Jasper wouldn't murder the person who could give him alibi, and anyway, why should he want to? Why should anyone want to? Who was she?"

"A retired social worker. Just a quiet little woman who seems to have been liked by everyone."

"And that's all she told Felix, that she'd seen Jasper on the stairs?"

"So he says."

"Then it must have been coincidence, unless she saw something more than she told Felix. Is that what you've got in mind?"

Since I did not know what I was supposed to have in mind, I took a moment to answer. Then, to have something to say, I replied, "If she did see anything more, I imagine no one will ever know what it was. Anyway, I don't know what there could be to see. The Farrars had taken over the top flat and Karen told Felix and me that Ted had some job he had to do on Sunday morning, but even if it had something to do with the flat, why should it matter if Miss Pace saw him?"

"Suppose she saw him with someone who couldn't afford to be seen with him?"

"Someone who came back later and murdered her? The brains behind the show whom you've been talking about? It couldn't have been Ted. Karen gave him an alibi. I know a wife's alibi isn't worth much, but in the mood she was in when I saw her I don't think she'd have invented one to help him. She thought he'd gone off to Singapore to join Audrey Beasley, leaving Karen with just thirty-seven pounds eighty-two pence in the world."

"Anyway, don't you think the job Ted had to do on Sunday morning was to come down here and murder Marcus?" Rose said. "Whether he was acting on his own or under somebody else's orders. Leaving the bracelet, I should think, was his own idea, an attempt to incriminate Jasper because of that old affair with Jill."

"Had Ted a bracelet?" I asked.

"I think so. At least, I know Jill had one. He could have used that. But I don't see where the death of your little woman fits in. I think it must have been coincidence. And, Virginia . . ."

"Yes?"

"Truly I'm sorry about the way I spoke to you this afternoon. I promise I won't do it again if you could bear to come and see me any time. It was just that I was upset that you could think Roland might ever have done anything that he could be blackmailed for, something not completely honest and generous and decent. He's been so good to me, Virginia, I owe him so much."

"I'm sure you're right. I'm very sorry I said what I did. Good-bye, Rose."

"Good-bye."

We rang off.

The next person whom I ought to telephone, I thought, if I was to keep my promise to Felix, was Roland Straker, but I was most unwilling to do it. I did not like the feeling of floundering around in the dark, not understanding what it was I was doing. While I was hesitating I began to think about Rose's suggestion that Lilian Pace had seen something more on the staircase at Little Carbery Street than she had told Felix about. Had she seen someone going up or coming down the stairs with Jasper Noble who could not afford to be seen there? My earlier suspicion of Roland Straker revived and I wondered if he had any alibi for the time of Lilian Pace's murder.

At last, however, I picked up the telephone directory, looked up his number and dialled it.

I was answered by his manservant, whom I remembered as a neat little man who looked after his employer with courteous efficiency. For a moment I was tempted to ask him if he could tell me anything about the whereabouts of Mr. Straker last Sunday, but was saved from doing anything so absurd by his saying immediately that he would fetch Mr. Straker.

A moment later Roland Straker said, "Yes, Mrs. Freer?"

I had thought out roughly what I meant to say.

"I don't know if I ought to bother you, Mr. Straker," I said, "but d'you remember we were talking about Jasper Noble this afternoon? You thought it was possible he might have killed Marcus Avery."

"Ah, yes," he said, "and I had a feeling you didn't agree with me."

"I wasn't convinced, though I'm not sure why," I said. "But now I've heard something which clears him completely and I thought perhaps you'd be interested in it."

"Of course I should," he said. "I'm interested in everything that touches Rose, as I'm sure you understand."

"Yes, but this hasn't any direct connection with her. My husband told me about it. It seems that on Sunday morning a woman called Lilian Pace, who lived on the ground floor of the house in Little Carbery Street, where he lives, and where

Audrey Beasley rented the top flat for a time, saw Jasper Noble come downstairs. And if he was in Little Carbery Street on Sunday morning, he can't have been in Allingford, murdering Marcus."

"I see," he said. "Well then, it seems certain we can cross him off our list of suspects. You're sure about this?"

"My husband seems sure," I answered. "She told him about it and I expect he's told the police. She couldn't do that herself because—but perhaps you've heard about that already."

"I haven't heard about anything. What did you say her name was?"

"Lilian Pace."

"It doesn't mean anything to me. Has something happened to her?"

"Yes, she was murdered herself that evening."

"She was—? No! You can't mean that! Murdered?"

"Yes, she was found choked to death in her flat by one of her neighbours."

"But that's terrible—terrible, Mrs. Freer. The poor woman. Choked to death, you say? You mean he used his hands to do it." His voice had turned hoarse with a horror that sounded genuine. There was a pause, then he went on, "Is there supposed to be any connection between her death and Marcus Avery's?"

"I believe the police are inclined to believe she was killed by a burglar and that there's no connection between the two things," I said. "But of course I don't know what they really think."

"No, naturally not. But she saw Noble in the morning, you say?"

"So I understand."

"Yet yesterday evening in the Rose and Crown he told us he'd been at home, indeed in bed, all that morning."

"I know."

"It's strange, isn't it? Doesn't it seem strange to you?"

"Very strange."

"Of course, he's a strange young man, or so I thought. Neurotic. Difficult to get along with, even if, as Rose tells me, he's really gifted. By the way, have you had any further contact with her since I spoke to you about her?"

"I've had a long talk with her on the telephone," I said. "I think we're friends."

"Good. I'm very grateful. I knew I could count on you. And thank you for giving me this information about Noble. It's very strange, but it's interesting. All the same, it looks to me now as if someone made a bad mistake when he left that bracelet on the scene. As you know, I was inclined to think the murder was Marcus's past catching up with him, that it was connected somehow with the time he'd spent in prison, some enemy he made or something he found out then and was perhaps trying to use. But, as you pointed out to me, the bracelet restricts the number of suspects to quite a small group of people."

"Rose thinks it may have belonged to Edmund Farrar's wife."

"Indeed? Then perhaps it won't be long before he's arrested."

"I don't know if you've heard what's happened to him already," I said. "Do you know he was arrested at Heathrow for trying to smuggle heroin into the country inside that plastic foot of his?"

There was no answer. I suppose the silence did not really last very long, but any silence on the telephone has a way of seeming to extend indefinitely.

"Mr. Straker . . ." I began.

"Yes, yes, I'm here," he said. "I was just trying to think out what it all means. And about that poor woman, too. Murdered. Horrible, and probably done without any remotely rational motive. Things are so lawless nowadays. There's so much senseless violence. I hope she didn't suffer. And heroin inside Farrar's artificial foot. Extraordinary." He was sounding increasingly incoherent and I was on the whole relieved when he brought our talk to an end by saying abruptly, "Well, thank you for telling me all this, Mrs. Freer. I must think about it. Good night."

He rang off before I had time to say good night myself.

That night I was restless, falling asleep, then waking, then falling asleep once more, but only briefly, and in the intervals, when I thought that I was awake, remaining really in an only half-conscious state in which my mind was crowded with disconnected images. It seemed to me that I was thinking rationally, but in the morning I could remember very little more of it than of a fast-fading dream. Only one of my thoughts was still clear to me and that concerned Siegfried and the linden leaf that had been the end of him.

It had seemed to me clear in the night that, as Roland Straker said, the silver bracelet had been somebody's bad mistake. Somebody's linden leaf. It was going to lead to the identification of the murderer. And I did not think this simply because the dragons' heads on the medallions had made me think of Siegfried bathing in dragon's blood, though the association had obviously had something to do with the way my mind had worked. It was something else about the dragon that interested me. I might be quite wrong about it, but at least it might be worth while to find out if I could. When I had had breakfast I dialled Felix's number.

There was no reply. I let the ringing go on for a long time, in case he needed a little while to wake up and get to the telephone, but I knew that the truth was that he had probably gone out to his mysterious office before I had even got up. But I could not leave the matter there. It was possible that Karen could tell me what I wanted to know and her telephone number would certainly be the same as Audrey's had been. I had a note of it and looked it up and dialled. A sleepy-sounding Karen answered.

I told her, "This is Virginia Freer. I wondered, can you tell me Jasper Noble's address?"

"Thirty-two Grieve Street," she replied. "That's a turning out of Little Carbery Street."

"I remember it," I said.

"But his workshop's in the basement under our shop. That's on the corner at the other end of Grieve Street. Do you want his telephone number?"

"I don't think so. Where is he likely to be in the morning? At home or in his workshop?"

"Oh, at home, for sure. He hardly ever gets up before about midday. He likes to work at night. That suited Ted, because Jasper was never in his way when he was about himself. Jasper had his own key to the place, of course, and generally turned up just about when Ted was leaving."

"Karen, I've heard about your husband being arrested," I said. "Felix told me."

I was not sure if the sound I heard was a sigh or a yawn.

"I've been such a fool, haven't I?" she said. "Thinking he'd gone off with that woman when he'd never given the slightest sign of even being interested in her. But when he actually told me he was joining her, well, what was I to think? And if the police hadn't caught him, I'd have believed he'd simply changed his mind and wanted to come back to me. And now I'm in such a muddle, I can't decide if I'm happy because he wasn't really leaving me for another woman, or unhappy because I suppose drug smuggling is really a rather awful thing to be mixed up in and it may mean he'll go to prison for years. Felix has been wonderfully kind. He seems to understand the way I feel. He doesn't think it's peculiar to have opposite feelings at the same time. He's a very understanding man, isn't he?"

"Oh, very." I did not think there was any need to warn her

that it was just that power of understanding that could make
Felix, when he gave his mind to it, such a dangerous con
man. She had no assets that I knew of on which he could be
tempted to prey, though what she said next made me uneasy.

"He's talking of giving me a job," she said. "I shall need
one, of course, if they're going to put Ted in prison. But he
never meant to leave me stranded with just thirty-seven
pounds eighty-two pence. If he'd got home safely he'd have
brought back lots of money and I'd never have known he
hadn't been in Yorkshire. He never really meant to be unkind
to me."

"What sort of job has Felix offered you?" I asked.

"Oh, just a secretary sort of thing," she answered. "We
haven't really gone into it."

As ignorant about the matter as before, I hoped it was
not something that was going to get the poor silly girl into
trouble.

"Well, thank you for Jasper's address," I said. "Good-bye."

I rang off, cleared away my breakfast and, as luckily I had
no appointments that day, got the car out of the garage and
set off for London.

Grieve Street was very like Little Carbery Street, a mixture
of fairly recently built, grim-looking office blocks, interspersed
with portions of not very distinguished Georgian terraces, but
there were more shops in it than in Little Carbery Street, in-
cluding an Indian restaurant and a fish and chip shop. I drove
along the street but could find nowhere to park, so in the end
I left my car in Little Carbery Street and walked back to
Grieve Street.

Number 32 was a small greengrocer's with boxes of fruit
and vegetables piled up outside it on the pavement, an incredible mass of goods packed as tightly as they could be jammed
together inside, and a plump Pakistani woman behind the
counter. There was a door to the left of the shop that had no
number on it but had a row of doorbells beside it, some of

which had cards tacked up next to them, and I thought that Jasper Noble's name might be on one of them. When I looked at them, however, it was not there. I wondered if Karen had absent-mindedly given me the wrong address, but when I went into the shop and asked the Pakistani woman if he lived there, she nodded and said, "Alfredo Moro."

"Oh, is that his real name?" I asked.

"No, no, Alfredo Moro live there before Mr. Noble," she answered. "But the bell don't work. You push the door and go in. Mr. Noble live on third floor."

I thanked her and went back to the street and, looking at the row of bells again, checked that Alfredo Moro had once lived on the third floor. His card was very faded. How long Jasper Noble had lived there without troubling to change it for one of his own I could not guess, but it seemed to me, from the little I had seen him, that it was in character that it should not have occurred to him to do this simple thing.

I pushed the door open and started up the steep, dark staircase, which was covered in treacherously worn linoleum. The smell was very like the smell of the staircase in the house in Little Carbery Street, a compound of sheer age and indifferent plumbing, but here it was complicated by a strong smell of curry, which seemed to seep out through the door that I passed on the first landing. The higher I climbed the dirtier the staircase became and the more chipped the paint. The door on the third landing had almost no paint left on it and looked so shrunken and loose in its frame that I thought it would open if I merely shook it.

It had no doorbell and no knocker. It had a letter-box, but a morning paper was still sticking in it, which suggested that Jasper had not yet got up to collect it, and I could not rattle the flap until I had pushed the paper all the way in. When I had done this and heard it drop on the floor, I made as much noise with the flap as I could and waited. There was no sound from inside. After a little while I rattled the flap again, and again there was no answer. If it had not been for the newspaper I should probably have assumed that Jasper, whatever his custom was, had for once got up and gone out already. After all, he had done this last Sunday morning, whatever he might choose to say about it. But it struck me as unlikely that if he had gone out he would have left the paper sticking in the letter-box like that. I rattled the flap a third time.

This time there was a furious answer from just inside the door.

"Can't you stop that bloody racket? What the hell d'you want?"

Jasper flung the door open. He was wearing a red and black checked dressing-gown that just reached his knees, and I thought had nothing under it. His legs and feet were bare. But as usual he was wearing a silver bracelet. His curly brown hair, tumbled around his pale, good-looking freckled face, had not had a comb through it since he had got up, and there were bristles on his jaw. His eyes, though they were bleary, gave me his strange, hungry stare.

"Oh, it's you," he muttered in a sullen tone. "What's-your-name, Felix's woman. What d'you want?"

He did not seem to expect me to come in.

"I'm sorry if I've disturbed you," I said, "but I'd like to talk to you."

He only went on staring at me, as if he were wondering whether or not to let me talk to him. Then, still without moving, he said irritably, "Well, what is it?"

"If I could come in . . ." I suggested.

"Is it something important?"

"It might be."

He gave a slight shrug of his shoulders and stood aside to let me enter.

The door opened straight into a fairly large room that had an unmade bed in one corner with sheets on it that had not been changed for some time, and a big table in the middle, littered with rolls of paper, some of which had been spread out and covered with sketches. There were the remains of a meal on one corner of the table which looked like last night's supper rather than this morning's breakfast. Baked beans, I thought, to go by what had dried on to the plate, and a glass that had held beer. There were a few chairs in varying states of decay and an unexpectedly handsome Persian carpet on the floor. There was also a silver dragon on the narrow mantelshelf. It was Tarasque himself, not a mere engraving of his head and flame-belching nostrils, but tail and all, in the solid.

As always, the creature gave me a feeling of discomfort, a sense that he represented something deeply evil, though the mere fact that he could make such a strong impression on me must mean, I knew, that uncommon talent had gone into his creation. A door facing me stood open. Through it I could see a room hardly larger than a cupboard which was kitchen and bathroom combined. There were some clothes in a heap at the foot of the bed and Jasper gathered them up.

"I'll get dressed, if you'll wait," he said in his muttering way and disappeared into the kitchen, kicking the door shut behind him.

I strolled to the table and stood looking at the sketches. They were designs for various pieces of jewellery, some with the dragon's head on them, some without, and most of them only roughly done, mere beginnings of ideas that had not yet been fully developed. Some were very dusty, as if they had lain there for a long time. I was still standing there, looking at them, when Jasper returned.

He was in his usual jeans and more or less white shirt and had scraped a razor over his chin, plainly too hurriedly, for there was a smear of blood on one side of it and a good many bristles had survived. Seeing me at the table seemed to annoy him, for he strode to it, swept the sheets of paper together and tossed them into a corner of the room.

"These aren't anything," he said. "Just mucking about. What d'you want?"

He threw himself down in a chair. Then it seemed to occur to him that as host he ought to offer one to me and, jumping up, said, "Sit down," then sat down again.

I did not sit down but walked to the hearth and drew a finger down the spine of the silver dragon.

"About this creature . . ." I began.

He interrupted at once. "Look, didn't I tell you the other night it doesn't mean anything special? You said something about its being a symbol of sin. Balls. I just happen to like it and it's become a sort of trade mark of my work. When I form myself into a limited company I'll have a picture of it in the heading of my notepaper. Does that satisfy you?"

"I don't mind what you do with it," I said. "I just wanted to ask you a more or less technical question."

"Technical? What do you know about it? Have you ever watched a silversmith at work?"

"Never. I don't know the first thing."

"Well, as long as you aren't going to talk about the golden apples of the Hesperides . . . Didn't you say a dragon was supposed to guard them?"

"Did I? You seem to have remembered more about that conversation than I have."

"I've a good memory. You said it sounded as if that dragon was mixed up in police work."

"Did I really? It wasn't a very clever thing to say. All I want to know now is whether all these dragons' heads of yours on your jewellery are the same."

"Are they exactly the same, do you mean?"

"Yes, or do they vary a little?"

"They vary quite a lot. I don't work from a transfer."

"And can you tell one from another?"

"I haven't thought about that but, generally speaking, yes, I should think so."

"You know the broken bracelet they found under Marcus's body?"

"Yes."

"Did the police show it to you when they arrested you?"

"They didn't arrest me. They only took me in for questioning."

"Yes, I'm sorry, that's what I should have said. Well, did they show the bracelet to you?"

"As a matter of fact, they did."

"And did you recognize it? Could you remember whom it had been sold to?"

"I could, but what business is it of yours?"

That was an awkward question, because I was not sure that it was my business at all. I seemed to have been pulled into the affair, but only through knowing other people who were much more deeply involved in it than I was. I decided to ignore the question, trusting that his curiosity as to what I was aiming at would make him answer mine.

"Whom did you sell it to?" I asked.

"To Rose."

"Rose! Rose herself, do you mean, or do you mean it was one of the things the Averys had in their shop?"

"I think Rose bought it for herself. She paid me for it. They didn't normally buy the things of mine they had in the shop. They just displayed them in that glass case of theirs and took a commission when they sold anything."

"And the one the police found was the one Rose had bought and paid you for?"

"Yes."

"Did you tell that to the police?"

"Yes."

"And they believed you?"

"Why shouldn't they?"

"I thought they believed it was your own and that the one

you've been wearing since then is a substitute. They didn't know, when they picked you up, that you had an alibi."

"An alibi . . ." His features tightened. "But I hadn't."

"You had. Didn't Lilian Pace see you on Sunday morning? And it happens that she mentioned that to Felix and he told me and I've told two or three other people, so now quite a number know you were in Little Carbery Street then and couldn't have murdered Marcus in spite of the attempt to incriminate you with that bracelet, and none of us can understand why you won't admit it."

Things happened so fast then that at the time I did not take them in, though later I realized that the expression I saw on Jasper's face was one of violent panic. For an instant he looked terrified. But then the terror changed to rage, his pale face flushed crimson, he shot up to his feet and shouted at me, "Get out! D'you hear me, get out, get out, get out!"

I was frightened. It seemed to me that the man had turned suddenly into a raving maniac and I was ready to do as he told me as quickly as I could. But once I was out of the room and standing at the top of the squalid staircase, I felt there was something I still had to say to him. I turned to face him.

"Do you know your friend Ted Farrar was arrested at Heathrow yesterday morning for trying to smuggle heroin into the country inside that plastic foot of his?" I asked.

He looked at me blankly. Then I saw disbelief on his face. Then he smiled. It was a smile of an unspeakably unpleasant sort of satisfaction, and it sent a shiver through me. I turned and started quickly downstairs. My heart was beating faster than usual and I had to resist a temptation actually to run down to the street. For some reason it was a relief when I heard the slam of his door upstairs. and not his footsteps behind me.

By the time I reached the street I had recovered. I had even come to the conclusion that there is something exhilarating about disliking someone intensely. It is pleasantly uncomplicated. Usually when I find myself disliking someone I feel at least a little guilty. I feel that my revulsion must be due to some failure of understanding on my part, that I have been oversensitive, or perhaps envious, and that I ought to take special pains to be nice to the person in question the next time we meet. But to feel complete conviction that someone to whom I have been talking is truly perfectly detestable brings with it a sort of peace. I was feeling quite calm when I turned into Little Carbery Street to return to my car and came face to face with Felix.

Usually when we meet he looks fairly pleased to see me, but that day he did not.

"What on earth are you doing here?" he asked as if I had no right to be walking along a London street.

"I've been to see Jasper," I said.

"For God's sake, why?"

I felt irritated. My calm mood evaporated.

"Didn't you tell me to tell as many people as I could about Miss Pace having seen him on Sunday morning?"

"But I didn't mean you to tell Jasper. You could have left that to me." He gave me a shrewd look. "Don't tell me that was the only thing that brought you to London."

"No, as a matter of fact, it wasn't," I said.

His ill humour seemed to fade. He put an arm through mine.

"Well, come up to the flat and have some lunch and tell me about it," he said.

I let myself be led along. "Do you usually come home for lunch?" I asked.

"Sometimes."

"Then your office is quite near, is it?"

"Not very, but I make my own hours. I shan't be going back to it this afternoon. That's the advantage of being boss."

"Do you mean you employ several people?"

"No, I don't. I suppose I should have said it's the advantage of being my own boss."

"You don't employ anybody?"

"Not at present."

"But Karen told me you'd offered her a job."

"When did you see Karen?"

"I haven't seen her. I only rang her up to ask her for Jasper's address. I tried ringing you first, but you were out, so I tried her. And she told me you'd offered her a job."

"Well, somebody's got to do something for her, haven't they? The poor child's quite lost. And that news yesterday about Ted's arrest—it's broken her up completely."

"I didn't think she sounded as if it had," I said. "I thought she sounded almost pleased that he hadn't actually gone off with another woman but was merely involved in a little thing like drug smuggling."

"If only that was all it was."

We were climbing the stairs up to Felix's flat. He took his key out of his pocket as we went up, unlocked the door and went in.

Following him in, I said, "What do you mean, Felix?"

"He's been charged with Marcus's murder and the murder of a woman in Soho last week who was involved in this drug business. Bob Hazell told me it had happened, though it hasn't got into the press yet. Now I suppose you want a drink."

"I could do with one."

He went out to the kitchen and returned with a whisky for each of us, his very pale, but as he knew my tastes there was a good deal more authority in the one that he had made for me.

"You drink too much," he said as he handed it to me. "It worries me."

"I'll stop when you stop smoking," I said. I sat down and took a generous swallow of my drink. "I remember about that murder in Soho. I read about it in *The Times* one day last week before all these troubles of ours started. It said the police wanted to interview a friend of the woman's who had a beard and a limp. I thought at the time it sounded too good to be true. Beards can so easily be removed and limps can be counterfeited. All the same . . ."

"Yes?" he said as I hesitated.

"I know someone else with a limp about whom I've had some rather ridiculous suspicions," I said. "Somehow I connected drugs and a limp. It must have been reading about that murder that made me do it."

"The beard was false all right," Felix said, "but of course Ted's limp was genuine. And a woman who knew the girl who was murdered has identified Ted."

"What makes the police think he murdered Marcus?"

Felix lay down in his favourite position, flat on the sofa, putting his drink down on the floor beside him and lighting a cigarette.

"Oh, there was never much mystery about that," he said. "I was sure he did it almost from the start. Who else would have thought of planting that bracelet on the scene? Who else would trouble to try to incriminate Jasper? But the police got him by ordinary routine procedure." There was a hint of scorn in his tone. "There was nothing brilliant about it. No imagination, no penetration. They simply happened to find a witness who saw a man with a limp leaving the Averys' shop on Sunday morning. And he'd left his car in the car-park without paying the fifteen pence he should have and sticking the ticket on his windscreen, and it happened a traffic warden came round and spotted it and left a summons for him and of course made a note of the number of the car. Very careless work on his part. If you're going to break the law in a big way, you should take the trouble to be very law-abiding in small ways."

"Rose seems to believe Ted's been Marcus's supplier and

the brains behind the thing, if that's what you can call it," I said. "She thinks he murdered Marcus because he thought Marcus was an informer."

"So you told me," Felix said. "But if he thought that, I think he was wrong."

"You don't think Marcus was an informer?"

Felix was gazing up at the ceiling with a vague stare which meant that he was withdrawing into what he would want me to assume was deep thought, but which I believed was merely a dream in which nothing very active went on.

To interrupt the process before it had gone too far, I said, "I haven't told you why I went to see Jasper."

Felix turned his head a little to look at me. "No."

"I wanted to ask him if he could recognize the bracelet the police found under Marcus's body. They showed it to him, of course, when they took him in for questioning. And he said he could. Apparently all those dragons are slightly different. And he said he sold that bracelet to Rose. So you see it may not have been Ted Farrar who planted the bracelet. Picking him as the murderer before the police did their own sort of solid work on the job may have been just a lucky guess on your part."

If he thought this an insult, which he probably did, Felix decided to ignore it. But he raised himself suddenly on to an elbow, looking startled.

"Jasper sold it to Rose?" he said. "I don't understand, do you? We know she didn't do the murder. She'd an alibi. She'd been to church, where lots of people had seen her. But you think she may have planted the bracelet, do you?"

"She could have."

"Why?"

"I don't know."

"Did you tell her about Jasper's alibi?"

"Yes."

"And who else?"

"Just Roland Straker."

"Ah, yes, the man who was with Rose in the Rose and Crown. Is that all?"

"Yes, except that I told Jasper several people knew about it and he seemed to go almost mad with rage or fear or something. But when I told him about Ted having been arrested he smiled. He didn't say anything, he just smiled a perfectly horrifying sort of smile."

Felix nodded thoughtfully. It all seemed to mean something to him.

"And you haven't told anyone else?"

"There's no one else involved, is there?"

But even as I said it, I felt a strange chill run through me. All of a sudden I remembered that I had told Tim Dancey the story of Jasper's alibi. Not that it seemed important just then. He was not involved in the affairs of the Averys. But wasn't he? Hadn't he told me himself that it was he who had amputated Ted Farrar's foot? So they at least knew one another. And Tim seemed to have a surprising amount of money, even for a successful surgeon.

There must have been some change in my expression, for Felix said, "What is it?"

"Nothing," I said. "Nothing at all. What about that lunch you mentioned?"

CHAPTER 9

We ate ham sandwiches and apples, then I set off for home. I had a feeling that Felix was impatient to see the last of me. This was unusual and indicated, I thought, that he had a plan of some sort for that afternoon which he did not want me to know anything about. It worried me, because when Felix started to make secret plans I generally expected trouble. They might not be actually illegal, they might be merely irresponsible and unrealistic, but they had a way of leading to upsetting consequences. However, I was not inclined to interfere. I had not yet had time to think over what I had learnt from Jasper Noble in the morning and was glad, as I drove homewards, to be by myself.

I wanted to work out what it meant that the bracelet found under Marcus's body had belonged to Rose, always assuming that Jasper had told me the truth about that. But unfortunately another thought kept interfering, one which it happened I did not want to think about at all, so the time I spent getting to Allingford was not very fruitful. This thought was simply that Tim Dancey was one of the people who knew the truth about Jasper's alibi, but it disturbed me more than seemed reasonable. What did it matter if he knew about it? What did it matter if everyone knew? I had never understood why Felix attached such importance to it and I was not much interested in the matter myself. All the same, I kept thinking of Tim, though I tried hard to stop doing so, but after expelling him from my thoughts for a little while, I kept finding he was back again. I had never given him so much thought before.

I started to wonder where his money came from, for certainly he had more than it was easy to explain. But so have lots of people. They inherit it from rich aunts, or they invest cleverly, or they gamble successfully. They do not necessarily do it by smuggling drugs. Yet some of them do. My head began to ache and when I reached home about four o'clock I put the car away in the garage, went indoors and made myself some tea and swallowed a couple of aspirins with it.

I felt a certain inclination to try to get in touch with Tim and ask him if we could meet during the evening, but I did not know where to track him down at that time of day and I was not really sure if I wanted to see him. If I did, what could I say to him? Ask him if he had kept in touch with Ted Farrar after supplying him with an artificial foot? Ask him if any of that wealth of his, his comfortable service flat, his pied-à-terre in London, his expensive holidays, his beautiful clothes, were paid for in part by the sale of heroin? But it was all too ridiculous. Then, because something in me would not let me make up my mind about the matter, I changed my shoes, put on my gardening gloves and went out into the garden, hoping to distract my thoughts by doing a little weeding.

I was still at it about six o'clock, trying to extricate some long trailers of bindweed that had got tangled up with a honeysuckle, when I heard footsteps on the paved path that led round the house from the street to the garden and, straightening my back and looking round, saw pink-faced Sergeant Roberts approaching.

"Pretty little place you've got here," he remarked, standing still about two yards away from me and looking round. "Very nice. Manage it yourself?"

"Yes," I said.

"I've never cared much about gardens," he said, "but the

wife does. It's a nice hobby for her. We've no children, you see. Pity. We'd have liked a family."

I was rather astonished at hearing him talk about himself in this way and it made me feel strangely alarmed. I felt that he could only be doing it because he was putting off telling me what had brought him, and that if this seemed to him necessary it must be something very bad indeed.

"Shall we go inside?" I said. "It's beginning to get cool."

"Perhaps that would be best," he said.

I led him to the back door and through the kitchen into the sitting-room, kicking off my gardening shoes as we went and putting on some slippers. As I waited for him to explain what he was doing there I felt my heart begin to beat in the way that it had when I was hurrying down the stairs, thoroughly frightened, after talking to Jasper Noble.

He looked round the room and I thought that if he remarked that it was a nice room I might scream. But at last he said, "I've brought you some news which I'm afraid you may find distressing, but first I'd like to ask you a question. Were you in London today?"

"Yes," I said. "But this news—what is it?"

"It really isn't so very bad," he went on. "Upsetting, of course, but probably not serious."

"What is it?" I nearly shouted at him.

"It's just that Mr. Freer—he *is* your husband, isn't he?— he's in St. Anthony's Hospital, suffering from concussion."

"Concussion!" I exclaimed. "Felix? Whatever happened?"

"Unfortunately he isn't conscious," the sergeant said, "so he can't give us his own account of things, and sometimes with these concussion cases there's a permanent black-out of what went just before the blow, but I think we shall be able to unravel more or less what happened even if he can't help us much."

"A blow?" I said. "Then he didn't simply fall downstairs or

get knocked over by a car or anything like that? Don't tell me he's been fighting. That doesn't sound at all like Felix."

"He was hit over the head with a wooden mallet," the sergeant said, "outside the basement door of Mr. Farrar's shop. That at least is what we presume. He was found collapsed in the area with the mallet beside him. But I really believe you needn't concern yourself too much. They'll keep him in hospital for a few days, of course, because concussion can be tricky, but I don't think there's any doubt of his recovery."

"Sergeant," I said, speaking very clearly and incisively, "will you please tell me exactly what happened? What was my husband, so called, doing in the area of Mr. Farrar's shop? I shall take it quite calmly. I shall not become hysterical. But I want to *know*."

I do not often become hysterical, except occasionally when I lose my temper. Then I sometimes behave in a way that I later regret. But all that usually happens to me when I become excited is that my speech becomes more clipped than usual and I hold my head higher and my back straighter than I normally do. Sitting down now, I did not relax in the chair but remained very upright with my hands clasped together in my lap.

The sergeant sat down too.

"The fact is, Mrs. Freer," he said, "we don't know exactly what Mr. Freer was doing in the area, with the body of Mrs. Avery in the basement. She'd been manually strangled and the safe in the room was standing open and Mr. Noble is missing. Those are the facts we know for certain."

"Rose Avery killed?" I cried. I had promised to keep calm, but it was more difficult than I had expected. "Strangled? Like Miss Pace?"

He nodded heavily.

"But what was she doing there?" I asked.

"Our belief is that she went there with the intention of killing Mr. Noble. There was a long and extremely sharp kitchen knife lying on the floor beside her with blood on it, and there were drops of blood on the way to the door and up the steps to the street, so it looks as if she wounded him but didn't manage to finish the job. But that's only surmise."

"And you think he killed her before she could kill him?"

"We'll know more about that when we can talk to Mr. Freer. He may have been a witness of what happened."

"If he can remember it."

"Just so."

I stared at him, trying to make something of his expression, but he only returned my stare with amiable stolidity.

After a moment I went on, "Why did you come to see me?"

"Partly, as I said, to tell you your husband is in hospital," he answered, "and partly to ask you if you can tell us anything about what Mr. Freer may have been doing this afternoon. I believe you were with him in the morning."

"How do you know that?" I asked.

"You were seen by Mrs. Farrar from a window of her flat on the top floor of the house in Little Carbery Street, coming in with Mr. Freer. So we thought you and he might have discussed what he intended to do in the afternoon."

I shook my head. "As a matter of fact, I had a feeling he had a plan of some sort that he wanted to get ahead with, but that he didn't want me to know what it was. We had lunch together, then I came home."

"May I ask, why did you go to see him?"

"I didn't. I met him by chance as I turned out of Grieve Street. I'd been to see Jasper Noble."

"I presume you'd some special reason for that."

"Yes, it was just an idea I'd had about the bracelet you found under Marcus Avery's body. I wanted to ask Mr. Noble if he could tell one of his bracelets from another and, if he could, did he know whom he'd sold that particular bracelet to. He said he'd sold it to Mrs. Avery."

There was no surprise on his face. "And what did you make of that?"

I said, "You knew it!"

He only looked blank and did not answer, but waited for me to answer the question he had asked.

"I didn't know what to make of it," I said. "She didn't murder her husband, did she? We know he was dead before she got home from church. Yet it looks as if she may have planted the bracelet there after she found him. I thought it was put there by Edmund Farrar to incriminate Jasper Noble, but why should she try to put her own signature, so to speak, on the crime?"

"Doesn't it seem likely she didn't realize Noble could tell his bracelets apart, and it wasn't Noble she wanted to incriminate but Farrar? A complicated gambit, but I think she was a complicated woman, Mrs. Freer. She wanted it to look as if Farrar had tried to frame Noble because of Noble's affair with his wife. Farrar's wife had also one of those bracelets, which was no doubt in his possession. Mrs. Avery told us about that herself."

"Yes," I said, "she told me too. It looks as if she wanted to be sure we knew it." I had relaxed a little and my hands had stopped clutching each other. "Did she know Edmund Farrar was the murderer from the start?"

Again he chose not to answer. He stood up.

"Who knows?" he said. "I'll leave you in peace now. Thank you for your help. If you want to visit your husband, he's in Ward 5 at St. Anthony's. But I'm sure you've no reason for anxiety. He'll probably be quite himself tomorrow. But, to tell you the truth, it's a marvel he didn't get killed, the wallop he got. Talking of dragons, didn't you tell us you're okay if you bathe in dragon's blood? Perhaps he did that."

He grinned. I let him let himself out.

I believe I stayed absolutely motionless for some minutes

after he had left. I thought of Felix and that a loving wife would hasten straight to his bedside. But no one could mistake me for a loving wife and I was abominably tired. It had been a long and wearing day and, besides Felix, there was Roland Straker to think about.

I wondered if he knew yet of Rose's death and whether or not I ought to telephone, or even go to see him. I felt terribly sorry for him because, as I began to think I understood Rose better, I believed her more than I had before, that he was a really good man and that he was deeply in love with her. And if hardly anything else that she had told me was true, at least she had been sincere when she protested passionately that he was too good for her. But I recoiled in fright from being the person who broke the news of her death to him, while I felt sure that if he knew of it already he would not want me around. At last, unlocking myself from my rigid posture and realizing how hungry I was, I went out to the kitchen and warmed up a frozen chicken pie that was in the refrigerator, ate it in the kitchen, then packed a small bag, got the car out of the garage once more and started the drive back to London.

St. Anthony's is one of London's oldest hospitals. Most of it is inexpressibly dreary with walls of dingy cream and passages of concrete which are flanked by inhospitable-looking benches on which solitary figures sit here and there, huddled and wretched in the exhaustion of anxiety as they wait for news of someone, news good or bad, but always seeming interminably long in coming. Here and there a ward has had a face-lift and through an open door it is possible to see pretty pale blue curtains and counterpanes and clean white walls, but these only make those endless corridors more depressing. In one of them, crouching alone on one of the benches, like all the other waiting figures I had passed, I found Karen Farrar.

I stopped when I saw her and said, "Hallo, Karen."

Her eyes had been shut, but they sprang wide open when she heard me and, lifting her head, she threw back her long, pale gold hair, which had fallen forward over her face. She flushed slightly as she looked at me.

"It's no good, they won't let you see him," she said. "I don't know why I've waited. He isn't conscious."

I had had some difficulty talking my way in as far as this, because visiting hours had been over for some time and only my insistence that I was the patient's wife and had been summoned from far off in the country by the police on purpose to see him had got me past a watchful character at the entrance. Karen, I supposed, must have come in much earlier and somehow been overlooked when the time came to leave. Or perhaps she had been allowed to stay because Felix's condition was far more serious than Sergeant Roberts had told me. In any case, having come so far, I did not mean to give in too easily and went to the doorway of Ward 5 and waited there for a nurse to take some notice of me.

After a moment a fresh-faced young girl came up to me and asked me what I wanted. I told her that my husband, Felix Freer, was in the ward and that I hoped I could see him. She said, "Oh yes," and that she would fetch Sister. The sister came after a little and I repeated why I was there.

She gave a slight shake of her head.

"I'm sorry, Mrs. Freer," she said, "he isn't conscious. And there's a policeman sitting with him in case he comes out of it and can talk. If I were you I'd go home and come back in the morning. Don't worry about him, he's going to be all right, but there's no telling how long he'll stay as he is. You might sit here for hours, all to no purpose. I really would go home."

Her face and her voice were kind. I thanked her and returned to Karen.

I told her what the sister had said and she stood up wearily and set off down the long corridor. She did not speak and she looked immensely dejected. In the street she stood looking around vaguely for a bus-stop, but I told her my car was nearby and that I could drive her home. I had decided to spend the night in Felix's flat. Even after all the years that he and I had been separated and although I had never made any use of it, I still had a key to the flat on my key-ring. I had thought from time to time that I ought to return it to him— as, for one thing, I had never let him have a key to my house —but I had a way of forgetting to do it. I am sure this was symbolic of something and would have told a psychologist something interesting about me, but I had never pondered the matter deeply. That evening it was convenient that I had the key. It would save me the expense of a hotel.

On the drive to Little Carbery Street Karen was almost silent. I wondered how far she had become involved with Felix and hoped for her own sake that she merely thought of him as a kindly support when she needed one and did not hope for much more than that. Felix could be very kind if not too much was expected of him, or for too long, but his attention soon strayed if demands went deeper. When we reached the door of his flat and I was fumbling in my handbag for my keys, she stood still instead of going on to her flat above, then blurted out, "May I come in and talk to you for a little while?"

"Of course," I said and led her into the flat. The May evening had become very cool and I switched on the electric fire in the living-room. "Would you like tea or coffee or anything?"

"No, thank you, please don't bother." She flopped down into a chair. "It's just that I somehow don't feel like being alone."

I noticed that she had washed her feet since I had seen her last and put fresh varnish on her toe-nails, but she was still wearing the flowered cotton dress, the only garment in which I had ever seen her, with a short velveteen jacket over it.

"D'you think they're telling us the truth?" she went on. "I
mean that he's going to be all right?"

"I'm sure he'll be all right," I said. "Felix always comes out
all right."

"He's been so good to me," she said. "I don't know what
I'd have done without him. First of all thinking Ted had left
me for that woman, and then finding out what a crook he
was. More than just a crook really. A murderer. I heard about
that this afternoon. I wasn't sure whether or not to believe it,
but they say he's actually confessed. It's all so strange, I can't
get it into my head. I was very happy with him, you see. He
was nice to live with. Do you think other murderers have
been nice to live with?"

"Some of their wives have been very loyal to them," I said,
"so I suppose they must have been." It intrigued me that
when she spoke of Audrey acid came into her voice, as if her
husband really had gone away with her.

"It's all such a muddle," she said with a sigh. "And I suppose if Felix doesn't recover, or even if he takes a good while
to get over things, that job he offered me will fall through.
Not that that's the main reason I'm worried about him, but I
was looking forward to it. I thought it sounded interesting."

"Just what was it?" I asked.

"I'm not sure exactly what I was going to have to do," she
said, "except type letters—I can type reasonably well—and
look after his files and so on. I think I was just to make myself generally useful in that marriage bureau of his."

"His what?"

"His marriage bureau—isn't that the right name for it? It's
called Sunset Love Ltd."

"Just a minute," I said. "Felix is running a marriage bureau
called Sunset Love?"

"Yes, didn't you know that? It's a beautiful idea really. It
brings lonely old people together and gives them a wonderful
new life. He's told me that some of the letters of gratitude

he's had have literally made him cry. It's a very important service he's supplying."

I had never seen Felix cry in my life, but now I understood why he had been afraid that I would laugh at him if he told me what he was doing.

"He is, of course, uniquely qualified to guide people into happy marriages," I said. "What does he get out of it himself?"

"I'm not quite sure how it works," Karen said, "but I understand people pay some sort of deposit when they register and then the rest of the fee when he finds them a partner. But I don't think the money's really important to him. It's the people themselves he cares about."

She had still a great deal to learn about Felix.

"Well, I'm sure he'll recover and you'll find your job waiting for you," I said. "But if I might give you some advice . . ."

"Yes?"

"I think, as a precaution, I'd start looking around for another job for when this one folds up. Felix's projects don't always last very long."

She stood up. "I'd thought of that myself," she said, which showed she was not quite such a simpleton as she appeared. "But at least it will tide me over for the present. Thank you for letting me come in for a chat. I feel better now. Good night."

I saw her to the door and let her out. It was nearly one o'clock. I was dead tired and went straight to bed.

The first thing I did when I got up next morning was to telephone St. Anthony's to ask how Felix was. I was put through to Ward 5 and a different sister from the one I had spoken to the evening before told me that Mr. Freer was conscious, had eaten a good breakfast, had talked at length to a policeman who had been in to visit him, and that he would no doubt be very glad to see me if I came to visit him too. I asked how long he was likely to have to remain in the hospital, but she would not commit herself. Not long, she said, but in a voice which might have implied hours, days or even weeks. But at least it was clear that there was no further cause for anxiety, so I did not hurry to get to the hospital but had a leisurely bath, made coffee and toast, took my time over my breakfast, then looked for a suitcase, packed it with Felix's pyjamas, dressing-gown, slippers and toilet things, and did not leave the house until half past ten.

The morning was sunny and calm. The little of the sky that it is possible to see in London above the rooftops was a pale but brilliant blue. Passing a flower shop in front of which there chanced to be parking space, I stopped on an impulse and bought a bunch of red tulips. Then I went into a tobacconist's which was next door to the flower shop and bought a packet of Felix's favourite brand of cigarettes.

Visiting hours had begun by the time I reached the hospital. Curtains had been drawn back from the cubicles that they formed when anything dreadful or merely intimate was being attended to and a few people sat beside beds here and there, holding muttering conversations with their occupants. Felix was at the far end of the ward. He was wearing a white hospital smock and had a dressing on his forehead but, except that he was paler than usual, he looked his normal self. I kissed him and deposited the tulips and the cigarettes on the locker beside him. As always good-mannered, he said the tulips were charming before reaching greedily for the cigarettes.

"You know, Virginia, you're a much nicer woman than you think you are," he said as I lit one for him.

"How are you?" I asked.

"I've a hell of a headache and I think I may be very ill," he said, "but they tell me I'm not."

"When are they going to send you home?"

"They haven't told me yet. Anyway, there'd be no one there to look after me."

"I think you can count on Karen to do that. They tell me you've been talking to the police."

"That's right, I have. Never-endingly, so it seemed to me."

"So suppose you talk to me and tell me how all this happened."

"Through my own lack of foresight. It was entirely my own fault."

"That doesn't tell me much."

He moved his head cautiously on the pillows that propped him up and blew a cloud of smoke in the air above him.

"Virginia, you're looking very lovely this morning," he said. "It really does me good to see you."

"I'm sure it does," I answered, "but I'd still like to know how you got yourself into this mess."

"I object to being told I've got into a mess," he said. "I've really come out of things pretty well. I might be dead."

I took the chair beside his bed. "I'm so glad you're not, but suppose you go back to the beginning and tell me why anyone should want to knock you so hard on the head."

"If I go back to the very beginning . . ." He paused and looked serious. "Perhaps I'd better do that, or you won't understand things. The beginning, from my point of view, was when Lilian Pace was murdered. I told you I wasn't much interested in Marcus's murder. Almost from the first I assumed Ted Farrar had done it, because who else, I thought, would have planted the bracelet there to frame Jasper? And the police, as I know now, knew from the first it was Ted, even before they'd found witnesses who saw him in Allingford. But they didn't arrest him because they wanted him to lead them first to his supplier in Singapore."

"How did they know it was Ted?"

"I'll come to that in a minute. I was wrong about his planting the bracelet, of course. Actually it didn't even occur to me Rose might have had anything to do with it. I'm not infallible."

"The police think Rose didn't realize Jasper could tell his bracelets apart and that she put it on the scene after she found Marcus dead because she wanted to make it look as if Farrar was trying to frame Jasper. She took pains to tell the police and me that Jill Farrar had had one of those bracelets, so that we should know Ted could have got hold of one."

"They're right," Felix said. "She was the brains of the organization, though Farrar did her killing for her. She got him to get rid of Marcus. But her reason for it had nothing to do with the drugs racket. It was simply because she wanted to shut it down and marry Roland Straker. He was a far better source of a safe and substantial income than the dangerous game she'd been playing with drugs. I've had an idea of that ever since I saw the two of them together in the Rose and Crown. She'd expected to have a quiet evening with him and she was very put out when he picked us up. More put out than seemed reasonable, I remember thinking. I think the way she worked things was to tell Farrar she'd found out Marcus was the informant who'd been telling the police so much about the movements of their little gang that they'd been getting picked up one after the other. I understand there'd been several cases of it that didn't get into the papers. And Rose thought first it was a girl in Soho who was doing it and Farrar murdered her to keep her quiet, but then they must somehow have found out they were wrong and Rose told Farrar she now knew it was Marcus and arranged with Farrar to put an end to him while she was safely in church. But as she was also aiming at putting an end to the whole gang so that she could settle down into respectability, she made that stupid blunder with the bracelet. She wanted to be sure the police got Farrar, after which, I suppose, she'd already planned to deal with Jasper herself, though all she did was tie herself in with the crime."

"So Jasper was in it too," I said.

"Of course he was," Felix said. "He was the informant."

"How do you make that out?"

"It's something I ought to have realized as soon as I knew that something seriously criminal, like drug smuggling, was connected with the murders."

"The murders? Both of them? Miss Pace as well as Marcus?"

"Yes, Jasper killed her because she saw him on the staircase."

"But she was his alibi," I said. "Why did he want to get rid of her of all people?"

"Because he was dead scared of being killed himself if he was found out by the gang. And he didn't need an alibi. The police knew he had nothing to do with Marcus's death. It was very stupid of me not to see that straight away. My main mistake was that I accepted Lilian's account of what she saw on Sunday morning. She told me she'd seen Jasper coming down from Audrey's flat. But think out what she actually saw. She was outside her own flat, which was on the ground floor, and she saw him come running down the stairs and he told her he'd been up to see Audrey and he rushed out of the house. And that was all. And, being a romantic old thing, she assumed he'd been up to Audrey's flat, as he said, yet actually she couldn't have known where he'd come from. Of course the person he'd really been to see was Bob Hazell. I think he'd been quietly feeding information to Bob for some time, and Bob had been passing it on to higher levels. And as long as Audrey was living in the top flat it didn't matter to Jasper if he was seen on the stairs because it would always be assumed that he was on his way to see her, as he was supposed to be violently in love with her. I doubt if he really was, but the appearance of it came in useful. Once she'd left the house, however, it was a different matter. If Lilian had told Ted Farrar about seeing Jasper there on the Sunday morning —and remember, the Farrars were just about to move into the top flat and she'd certainly have seen something of them and you know what a chatty old thing she was—Ted would have guessed at once what Jasper had really been doing, and Ted had already killed twice. Perhaps more often, for all we know. So Jasper would have known his days were numbered if she talked, and so—well, he silenced her."

"You were scared yourself when you heard she'd been murdered, weren't you?" I said. "That's why you wouldn't tell the police what she'd told you about seeing Jasper. You thought her murderer might try to silence you. But at the time you thought it was because Jasper was meant to be arrested for Marcus's murder, and she could upset that. What made you suddenly change your mind and decide to tell as many people as possible about it?"

"It was because of something you said to me," he answered. "You reminded me of that talk we'd had with Bob, when he agreed the police usually got people for things like smuggling on information received. It made me think about Bob and it suddenly struck me how stupid I'd been, believing that Jasper had been up to Audrey's flat when it was obviously Bob's he'd been up to, and that he was an informant whom the gang would deal with if they found out about him."

"But why did you want to tell as many people as possible about his having been there?"

"Bait," Felix said.

"I don't understand."

"I wanted to get Jasper for Lilian's murder, but also I thought I'd like to catch whoever had been at the back of the whole thing, because really that person was responsible for her death. Ever since you told me the bracelet had belonged to Rose I was fairly sure it was Rose, but I wanted to make sure and I thought if she heard about Lilian having seen Jasper she'd probably come after him. Even if he'd already told the police as much as he knew about her, he couldn't have given evidence against her if he was dead. Farrar could have talked, of course, but he'd really nothing to gain by it. He'd only dig himself further into trouble if he did. So that's why I didn't much want you staying around yesterday afternoon. I wanted to get on with the job. And if anyone ever wants me to eat curry again, I shall vomit."

"Why has curry come into the picture all of a sudden?"

"There's an Indian restaurant opposite the house where Jasper lived, and I went and planted myself there at a window for most of the rest of the day. I think the proprietor was puzzled, but he seemed resigned to my sitting there if I went on eating something, so I ate curry after curry and drank cup after cup of tea, watching for Jasper to come out, till I felt I was going to blow up. I knew he didn't often come out till the evening, but I thought he might make an exception for once, as he did last Sunday, a thing, incidentally, that Rose and Ted would not have expected. And I thought Rose would be watching for him from somewhere, like me, and would go after him, and that was the worst mistake I made, because she was waiting for him all the time in Ted's basement. She'd a key to the shop, since that was their headquarters, and all the money they'd been piling up was in the safe there, waiting to be distributed among them when they decided it was safe to start appearing rich. The police have known all about it all along from Jasper, of course. They've only been waiting to pounce on whoever came to collect it. I'm not sure if Jasper knew Rose was the boss. He may have believed it was Ted and that's why he smiled in the way you described when he heard Ted had been arrested at last. It must have made him feel safe. Anyway, Rose was there when I followed him to the shop and went down the area steps after him. I actually saw her through the window jump out at him and try to stab him. I think she wounded him, but she didn't kill him. He's pretty strong and I saw him knock her out. I was trying to get in at the door, but it was locked and I couldn't open it. And then something happened to me, I'm not sure what, because I can't remember anything after that. I think he heard me at the door and came out and hit me on the head, so that I passed out. Unfortunately I'm not much good at the tough stuff. I ought to have called a policeman. And then I think Jasper went back into the basement and strangled Rose and made off with all the money in the safe. Luckily he either thought he'd finished me off already, or that it wasn't worth waiting around to do it. Of course the police will get him pretty soon. He'll never get out of the country, if that's what he tries to do."

"What were the police doing while all this was going on?" I asked.

"Watching Rose, who must have known it and managed to give them the slip. And they weren't bothering about Jasper, because they thought he was working for them."

"I suppose when they arrested him at the beginning of all of this it was only to make the rest of the gang think they'd fallen for the business about the bracelet. I expect he told them then that it belonged to Rose."

Felix made a face of disgust. "Naturally. They knew almost everything. But they didn't understand about Lilian's death. They were inclined to think it was an ordinary break-in." He frowned. "Why are you smiling?"

"I didn't know I was," I said. "I was only thinking that the first time I met Jasper I told him a dragon was said to have guarded the golden apples of the Hesperides, and I said you might call that police work. It seemed to annoy him intensely and he remembered it when I'd quite forgotten about it. I suppose he was afraid I was hinting that I knew something about his undercover activities. Do you know if they caught the man in Singapore?"

He shook his head and winced at the movement. "They haven't told me. Somehow I don't think so. I'd guess it's a good sort of place to disappear in. But I'm not much interested any more. They've known so much all along, I really needn't have troubled myself about it as much as I did. All the same, they did need me to tell them the reason for Lilian's death. I managed to do that for her."

"So now that it's all over, you'll be getting back to your job," I said. "Karen tells me you're running a marriage bureau."

He gave me a quick look, then gazed up at the ward's lofty ceiling.

"Suppose I am," he said.

"She told me you were giving her a job."

"She needs one. And if I can teach her to dress a bit better she may even be useful."

I spoke, I thought, very sympathetically. "It sounds interesting. Just what do you do?"

"I find people husbands and wives. I specialize in old people. Lonely people. I don't see why you should sneer at me for doing that."

"I didn't think I was sneering," I said, "though I'm a little unsure about your qualifications. How did you get into it?"

"Through a man I knew who was running it, but he got into a mess and thought it best to fade out, so I took over his office and his mailing list and so on at a very modest cost, and I managed to raise a loan to cover it and I've been doing quite well. But I knew you'd only laugh at the idea that I could make a success of running a business of my own."

"It isn't the fact that it's a business of your own that makes me feel a little mirthful," I said. "It's the kind of business it is. How did your predecessor get into a mess?"

"Oh, he was a bit of a crook. He was taking the premiums his clients were paying him and not delivering the goods."

"And you do?"

His gaze avoided mine. "Whenever possible. Some people are very hard to please."

"Karen told me you'd had a letter of gratitude that had actually made you cry."

"Karen's a very sweet girl, but perhaps she exaggerates. I've had the letters of gratitude, but I don't think I've wept, though I admit I've sometimes felt like it. They can be very moving. I had one last week inviting me to tea with a couple I'd brought together. I think I told you about them. I had a delicious tea of crumpets and homemade sponge-cake last Sunday, just before going to see the Farrars and hearing about Marcus's murder and Jasper's arrest. Such a contrast. Peace and happiness and then all that misery. Those two were one of my successes. They were both seventy-five and both widowed and both had small but adequate incomes, and he could drive a car but couldn't cook, and she could cook but couldn't drive. And they both like watching the same television programmes and reading the same sort of crime stories, no violence, no sex, just a comfortable read before going to sleep. When I got their two application forms I knew I couldn't go wrong if I brought them together."

"I thought all that kind of thing was done by computer nowadays," I said. "You feed in the facts about someone and out comes the name and address of their perfect partner."

"Well, as a matter of fact, I do tell them it's done by computer," Felix said. "People have such faith in them nowadays and if you go wrong you can always blame it on a technical hitch. When I got my last bank statement it told me I'd an overdraft of forty-seven thousand pounds and when I pointed out to them they'd made a slight mistake they apologized and said it was all the fault of the computer, instead of having to admit that one of their staff put the decimal point in the wrong place. I feel quite sorry for those poor old computers, you know. They get blamed for everything."

"Then how do you actually manage things?"

"How do you suppose? I use intuition, insight, imagination. And it turns out all right over and over again. Once or twice I've stumbled across the fortune hunter, or the kind of person I feel might murder his brides in their baths, but I make short work of them."

"And that's why you tried reading up on psycho-analysis. You thought it might help you with this intuition of yours."

"Yes, but it works out better if I rely on my native abilities. I think Bob Hazell got me reading the stuff originally because he thought it might help me to understand myself. Funny—I don't know why he thought I couldn't manage that on my own. By the way"—he gave a sudden grin—"how's your marriage coming along? Anything I can do to help there? I told you, I specialize in the elderly. Their numbers are increasing so enormously and somebody ought to help them. But I don't mind a middle-aged case now and again."

"Thanks for the offer," I said, "but that's something I'll manage on my own."

But could I?

Driving home presently, I turned the matter over in my mind and recognized that there had never been the slightest chance that I would marry Tim Dancey, and I was thankful to be quite clear about the matter at last. I liked him, but I had actually frightened myself for a little while into half believing that he might be the brains behind Rose Avery's drug smuggling. And little as I trusted Felix in most things, I had never even dreamt that he could be any such thing. It showed how inadequate my understanding was of Tim.

If I had been younger this might not have mattered to me. His good looks, his intelligence, his good nature might have been enough to make me risk getting out of my depth. But three years of marriage to Felix had made an irremediable change in me. I would never again be ready to take a leap in the dark.

But that did not mean that I must see no more of Tim. It did not mean that I might not start taking a certain amount of trouble to get to know him better. As I drove on I found that a thought that was somehow encouraging.